Tharlo

Tharlo

Short story and film script by **Pema Tseden**

Published in 2017 by

MCCM Creations
www.mccmcreations.com

University Museum and Art Gallery
The University of Hong Kong
www.umag.hku.hk

Series editor: Christopher Mattison

Translator: Jessica Yeung

Book editors: Jessica Yeung and Wai-ping Yau

Film text editors: Pema Tseden, Jessica Yeung and Tsemdo

Editorial assistants: Tsemdo, Yan Lai and Nick Lin

Photographer: Tsemdo

Calligrapher: Pema Tseden

Book designer: fangönei

ISBN 978-988-77238-3-7

Contents

>> Introduction

The Films and Fiction of Pema Tseden[1]

Jessica Yeung and Wai-ping Yau

PEMA TSEDEN

Born in 1969 in the Tibetan area of Amdo in Qinghai Province, China, Pema Tseden began his career as a fiction writer and literary translator at Northwest University for Nationalities, later becoming the first Tibetan to graduate from the Beijing Film Academy. He attracted critical attention for his student shorts *The Silent Holy Stones* (2002) and *The Grassland* (2004), both shot on location in Amdo with a cast of amateur Tibetan actors. His first documentary *The Weatherman's Legacy* (made for Discovery Channel Asia, 2004) was followed not long after by his first feature-length film *The Silent Holy Stones*, a 2006 remake of his student short of the same name. Meanwhile, he continued to write and in 2006 published a co-authored book in Chinese with Wangshik Tseden titled *The Master in Tibet*, about Padmasambhava, the holy man who converted Tibet to Buddhism. In 2007 Pema Tseden made his second feature film *The Search* and two Chinese-language documentaries *Kathok Puja* and *Samye Monastery*. In 2008 he directed the television film *Flapping Flares in 1983* for the China Movie Channel. This has been his only Chinese language feature film, and the only one not set in an area of Tibet, and based on a script that he did not write. In 2009 he published his first collection of short stories written in Tibetan, *Temptation*, as well as a translation into Chinese of a collection of Tibetan folklore titled *Unending Stories*. His fourth feature, *Old Dog*, was released in 2010. His stature as a writer and translator grew with his first collection of short stories written in Chinese, *Dreams of a Wandering Singer* (2011); a collection of short stories written in Tibetan, *City Life* (2012); and a translation into Chinese of Tibetan writer Takbum

---

[1] An earlier version of sections of this preface on Pema Tseden's films was published in *The Journal of Chinese Cinemas* 10(2), 2016, and on his short stories in *Soochow Academics* (4), 2015.

Gyal's short stories, *Songs of Life* (2012). Pema Tseden's fifth feature *The Sacred Arrow* was released in 2014. This same year saw the publication of his second collection of short stories written in Chinese, *Holy Stones, Quietly Chiseled*, the second edition of *Unending Stories* (retitled *Tibet: Unending Stories*) and a collection of previously published and new short stories written in Chinese, *The Colour of Death*. His sixth and latest feature, *Tharlo*, released in 2015, holds an important place in Pema Tseden's work, not solely because it has been the most successful in terms of international awards and festival screenings, but also because it is the first Tibetan-language film to receive theatre release in Mainland China. In addition, it has been the most comprehensive expression of the themes and motifs that recur in his oeuvre. In terms of narrative and cinematographic experimentation, *Tharlo* also shows a level of detail and confidence unseen in his previous films. In 2016 Pema Tseden brought together previously published and new short stories written in Chinese in a collection named after the short story from which the film *Tharlo* is adapted.

READING PEMA TSEDEN'S WORKS AS PALIMPSESTS

Pema Tseden's creative output may be most productively read as palimpsests, a notion that allows an insight into the ways in which images, scenes, characters, actions and relationships from his previous works are constantly revisited and unpredictably transformed into new constellations, so that a new layer of meaning emerges with each iteration.[2] A palimpsestic reading shows Pema Tseden's oeuvre to be attempts to open up lines of questioning that resist narrative closure, dissolve dichotomies such as tradition and modernity or the spiritual and the mundane, and draw attention to the unfixity of the self and the diversity of perspectives. Moreover, analysing these films and short stories as palimpsests provides a key to understanding the ways in which

---

[2] This introduction will focus on Pema Tseden's feature films and not his television film *Flapping Flares in 1983*. The film's producer Li Xing noted in a telephone interview with the editors that the parameters for that production had already been set by the time Pema Tseden was engaged as the film's director. As such, the film falls outside of Pema Tseden's auteurist repertoire.

a sense of bleakness in Tibet, and in life in general, is accompanied by a utopian impulse springing from a compassionate view of the world that is an essential part of Buddhism. Examining Pema Tseden's revisitations in the context of the social and political reality of contemporary China, it is argued, enables the exploration of ways in which his works disturb popular images of Tibet, address issues of identity and articulate the problems and aspirations of Tibetans, and also of humanity generally, in the challenges of existence.

FILMS

The palimpsest is used by Gérard Genette (1997, 5) as an analogy for hypertextuality, an aspect of textuality that refers to the ways in which a text (called a hypertext) is derived from a prior text (hypotext) through a transformative process. For example, *Ulysses* and *The Aeneid* are hypertexts of the same hypotext—*The Odyssey*, though in different ways—'Joyce extracts from it a pattern of actions and relationships, which he treats altogether in a different style', whereas 'Virgil appropriates a certain style, which he applies to a different action'(6). Whether it is a style or a pattern of actions and relationships, 'a new function is superimposed upon and interwoven with an older structure' (398). It is this 'making of new things out of old' that the notion of the palimpsest aims to capture: 'on the same parchment, one text can become superimposed upon another, which it does not quite conceal but allows to show through' (398–9). While frequently associated with literary texts, the notion of the palimpsest also lends itself to cinema: Woody Allen's 1972 film *Play It Again, Sam*, a reworking of Michael Curtiz's 1942 film *Casablanca*, is a case of 'cinematographic hypertextuality' (156). Robert Stam (2005, 31) suggests that film adaptations can be productively understood as 'hypertexts derived from pre-existing hypotexts which have been transformed by operations of selection, amplification, concretization, and actualization'. Hypertextuality provides a useful framework for analysing Pema Tseden's works, not only because his first feature *The Silent Holy Stones* is a remake of his 2002 student short of the same name, and his latest film *Tharlo* is an adaptation of his 2012 short story of the same name, but also because a palimpsestic reading reveals that Pema Tseden's revisitations of his previous works are driven by a desire to open up possibilities for understanding Tibetan culture in the context of contemporary China, and issues of identity, modernity and compassion in the contemporary world.

The Grassland

Pema Tseden's graduation short *The Grassland* (2004) revolves around a Tibetan herding community scandalised by the theft, by a young herdsman, of a yak which has been set free as an act of religious merit. This theft is especially outrageous because it is not the first time that such sacred animals have been stolen by a member of the younger generation. The theft of the yak is presented as an act of sacrilege, an appalling sign of the rift between the young and the old, a falling away from traditional cultural values, social hierarchies and religious practices. *The Grassland* follows the chieftain Tsedruk as he takes the old woman Ama Tsomo across the grassland to confront the young men suspected of stealing the yak she has set free; the culprit turns out to be Juga, son of the chieftain Dorlo. Ama Tsomo, however, is reluctant about the journey as she is concerned about bringing punishment to the thief, which would go against her compassionate intention of setting free a living creature.

The Grassland serves as a hypotext for Pema Tseden's later work in several ways. First, theft as the epitome of the erosion of Tibetan traditions will develop into a recurring motif in Pema Tseden's later films, where the gap between the generations grows ever wider as the traditional Tibetan way of life comes under siege from the egoism, materialism and irreligiousness unleashed by economic development. This motif of theft will be repeated in *Old Dog* (2010), where the object of theft is a Tibetan mastiff. In *Tharlo* (2015), the theft is committed by a materialistic young woman, and by the male protagonist in his attempt to run away with the woman.

Second, in *The Grassland* Tsedruk and Ama Tsomo meet an old stone carver on their way to confront the suspects; the relationships between the old stone carver and other characters will be transferred to *The Silent Holy Stones* (2006), and transformed into various possibilities for responding to the crisis of Tibetan culture.

Third, the opening sequence of *The Grassland* will be revisited at the end of *Old Dog*. This opening sequence is an exercise in style that exemplifies the fundamental principle of hypertextuality as a patterning of repetition and difference. As the credits open, the camera follows an eagle gliding across the sky, and then dissolves into an empty frame in such a way that the transition between the two shots coincides with the eagle's descent. As the eagle gradually disappears, the movement of the camera echoes its dip as it tilts down to show open grassland with a running stream in the foreground and mountains in the distance. The title of the film appears (in Tibetan, Chinese and English) at the precise moment when the grassland comes into view. The tilt-down is then followed by a pan-right along the stream in the foreground. As we struggle to pick out the black figure among the white sheep scattered across the grassland, the pan-right dissolves to a wide tracking shot that continues the rightward direction and enlarges the black figure, so that we can now see two people travelling towards the camera: one on the back of a yak, and the other on foot leading the animal by the nose. While the hat, the robe and the gait of the person walking suggest a man, it is hard to make out the person riding except for a head of grey hair. Next, the camera cuts to a lateral tracking shot framing the back of the man's hat and upper torso in medium close-up as he walks left to right. After a few steps, the man turns around, addresses the person riding (off screen) as Ama Tsomo, and assures, 'We're almost there.' Just as the man turns to face away from the camera, there is a cut to a lateral tracking shot that reverses the screen direction: the two characters are now shown travelling right to left. We hear an old woman's voice from Ama Tsomo (whose face is blocked by the man's hat) pleading, 'Just forget it. Let's turn back.' Then the full figure of Ama Tsomo comes into view, providing a sharp, ironic visual counterpoint to the man—not only is the grey hair matched by the furry beige hat, but the gentle rhythm with which Ama Tsomo turns the hand-held prayer wheel is echoed with great exaggeration by the man as he gesticulates with his hand to make his point, 'I shall get to the bottom of this matter.' This juxtaposition between the man's resolve and Ama Tsomo's reservations (about finding out who stole the yak set free by Ama Tsomo, we learn later in the film) is sustained through the next two shots (a cut to a medium close-up of Ama Tsomo turning her prayer wheel, followed by a cut to a medium close-up of the man, with Ama Tsomo briefly drifting in and out of the frame) to the end of the sequence when the two characters move out of the frame, leaving behind an empty sky. Through editing and mobile framing, this opening sequence puts into play a process of transformation, whereby an element emerges as other than itself as it is transferred from one context to another. From this process come new experiences, perceptions, perspectives, expectations and possibilities. The eagle's descent becomes a tilt-down that extends our spatial experience from the sky to a grassland with a stream running across it. The flow of the stream is taken up by the pan-right and the subsequent tracking shots, which enhance our perceptions of the man through the elaboration or revelation of details such as the face. The same face is seen from a different perspective when the camera cuts to a tracking shot that frames the man and Ama Tsomo in such a way that the blocked figure of Ama Tsomo is gradually brought into full view to create a counterpoint to the man. When the sequence ends with a return to an empty frame of the sky, expectations are raised about the two characters, and possibilities for development remain open. The sequence that opens *The Grassland* suggests a strong desire to explore different perspectives and possibilities, a desire that is present in all of Pema Tseden's films, and palpably so in the ending of *Old Dog*.

The Silent Holy Stones

Pema Tseden's 2006 feature *The Silent Holy Stones* is a hypertext of his 2002 student short of the same name, as well as of *The Grassland*. Scenes, characters and narrative events from these hypotexts are transformed to discover ways of understanding issues arising from a confrontation between tradition and modernity, between religious precepts and mundane practices.

In remaking the student short, the feature retains the same basic story line. A ten-year-old Buddhist novice nicknamed Little Lama finds himself drawn to the television dramatisation of the classic Chinese novel *Journey to the West*, watched on a VCD player on a two-day visit with his family during the New Year celebration. He is so fascinated by this dramatisation that he begs, successfully, for his father to bring the television set, the VCD player and the VCD box set of the drama to the monastery to share with his master (affectionately called Old Lama by others). The story ends with Little Lama chanting cheerfully in an assembly after his father promises to share the drama with the monks and novices again in the future. The feature has the same setting and the same actors playing major roles (such as Little Lama, Old Lama and Little Living Buddha), but there are also new layers of plot, backstories and additional characters.

One significant additional character is derived from the old stone carver in *The Grassland*, whose relationships with other characters are transformed into complex patterns of social interactions in *The Silent Holy Stones*. In *The Grassland*, Tsedruk (the man leading the yak in the opening sequence) and Ama Tsomo meet the old stone carver Zoba on their way to see the chieftain Dorlo. In this scene, Zoba is shown to be a deeply religious man devoted to his work, with a young girl in his care and a mastiff as his companion. Zoba is scandalised by the theft of the sacred yak, but is also impressed by Ama Tsomo's selfless compassion when she explains her reluctance to find the culprit: she no longer owns the yak the moment it is set free; moreover, and more importantly, the culprit will only suffer in prison (that is, possibly with little chance of rehabilitation). At the end of the scene, confronted with complex issues arising from the dissolution of the traditional way of life, the girl is shown standing against a background of fluttering prayer flags, with the faintest parting of her lips, as if wanting to say something urgent to the departing Tsedruk and Ama Tsomo. This scene is reproduced with significant differences in *The Silent Holy Stones*, when Little Lama and his father meet the old stone carver on their way home from the monastery for the New Year celebration. Here, the stone carver is also called Zoba, but is at a more advanced age, and without the company of a mastiff or a young child. The girl's close affinity with the old stone carver in *The Grassland* is transferred to Little Lama's admiration for the old man's art of stone carving: running his fingers appreciatively over the surface of a work in progress, Little Lama requests a holy stone, and is promised one carved with the six-syllable mantra.

But transference is not the only means of introducing difference. A backstory prompted by the conspicuous absence of Zoba's children in *The Grassland* is woven into the plot in *The Silent Holy Stones*. In *The Grassland*, the girl is unlikely to be a child of Zoba. But, if she is his grandchild, who and where are her parents? In *The Silent Holy Stones*, we are told that the old stone carver has a son who refused to inherit the craft of stone carving, and left home to seek success in Lhasa. Although he never appears in the film, it is this image of the son as a young man who turned his back on tradition to pursue material goals that provides a thread between two other additional characters—Little Lama's older brother and the drunk young man. The older brother has a keen business acumen that allows him to acquire wealth and symbols of technology, such as the motorbike, television set and VCD player. He enjoys dancing to disco music, but also plays the leading role in the Tibetan opera performance of the classic legend of the compassionate prince Drime Kunden during the New Year celebration. Thus, the older brother is associated with both traditional spirituality and an entrepreneurial drive. In this sense, the drunk young man functions as a foil: he shows a complete disrespect for his elders and disrupts the opera performance by blocking the audience and shouting dazedly to an actor on stage. Yet there is a curious relationship between these two young men: the drunk not only desires the older brother's girlfriend, but also addresses him as a potential drinking partner. A link between them is provided by the carver's son, who, like Little Lama's older brother, seeks wealth and appears to have achieved some success, and who, like the drunk young man, is faulted by his elders for failing to live up to tradition. The blurred boundaries between these characters suggest that—rather than fixed, finalised positions—these are possibilities and permutations created by a process of transformation that engages with an absence in an antecedent condition (that is, the absence of Zoba's children).

In *The Silent Holy Stones*, this emphasis on addition, alteration and amplification as ways of discovering new possibilities and perspectives is also evident in the portrayal of Little Living Buddha and Little Lama's younger brother. In the student short, the younger brother is completely marginal, while Little Living Buddha's role is relatively minor, mainly functioning as a playmate whose television set and VCD player (the only ones in the monastery) hold a special fascination for Little Lama. In the feature, Little Living Buddha is rendered into a double of Little Lama through a series of resemblances. On different occasions, both say that they have watched *Drime Kunden* many times (one refers to a television dramatisation, the other to a live performance); both ask if the destination is the same for Old Lama's pilgrimage and the Buddhist monk's trek in *Journey to the West*; and both wear a mask of the character Monkey King from *Journey to the West*. But of course Little Living Buddha's status is fundamentally different: he is told by his tutor to remove the Monkey King mask for being inappropriate. Little Lama is also attached to his religion, but has more freedom and flexibility in applying religious precepts to everyday life. It is this simultaneous capacity for attachment and ambiguity that distinguishes Little Lama from both his younger brother and Little Living Buddha. The younger brother is thoroughly materialistic. Whereas Little Lama learns Tibetan to read Buddhist scriptures, the younger brother is utterly uninterested. For him, mathematics is a passport to professional success, and fluency in Chinese means work opportunities in the big city. Thus, Pema Tseden's approach to remaking produces a spectrum of characters and their situations, which allows the plot to build on different patterns of attitudes, aspirations, thoughts and perceptions.

The plot is further driven by additional layers created by expanding two narrative events, each concerning the contemporary representation of a classic legend. In the student short, the television dramatisation of the legend of Drime Kunden is shown only once, briefly, and not very clearly, when it is watched by novices and monks in Little Living Buddha's quarters on New Year's Day. In the feature, novices and monks watch a New Year variety show instead, an indication of how popular culture has penetrated monastic life. But Little Lama and Little Living Buddha do watch the television dramatisation on the VCD player on their own on New Year's Eve. Because both are familiar with the plot, they skip the childhood episodes and fast forward to the best part, which begins with the prince opening the doors of the treasury to help the poor shortly before he is exiled by the king for harming the kingdom. Selecting this episode shows their grasp of the legend, where compassion is spoken of not simply as a sentiment, but as a practice, in this case pursuing social justice by providing for the poor even to the point of enraging the establishment. But it is also worth noting that they both laugh at the human figures in fast forward mode. The rapid mechanical movements are comical because, following Bergson (1911), they suggest the 'easy automatism of acquired habits' (19), as well as the lack of 'a constantly alert attention that discerns the outlines of a present situation, together with a certain elasticity of mind and body to enable us to adapt ourselves in consequence' (18). Laughter is a corrective to this lack. This implies that applying the insights of the legend requires us to pay close attention and to adapt to the present situation.

This is brought out in a refreshing way in a later scene where the actors rehearse for a live performance in Little Lama's home village for the New Year celebrations. There, the actors, all in jeans and jackets, play out the drama of Drime Kunden giving away his three children to three visitors who require them as servants. A shot taken from the back of the stage shows Drime Kunden (played by Little Lama's older brother) painfully parting with his only son and two daughters (one is played by Little Lama's younger sister), as Little Lama (in his monk's robe) and his younger brother (in jeans and jacket) watch off stage, with parked motorbikes in the background, calling attention to the fact that this drama is playing out in a contemporary context. Whereas the younger brother is seen sitting, distracted, on the edge of the frame, an attentive Little Lama is literally drawn into the drama, finding himself framed between Drime Kunden and his tearful children. Praising in particular his younger sister's moving performance, Little Lama clearly finds relevance and meaning in the drama, implying that its power to inspire transcends the trappings of staging or costuming, that its insight eludes a literal interpretation, and that poetry is what survives translation. That a rigid, literal approach to understanding the drama is unproductive is echoed later when the younger brother expresses reluctance to emulate the prince's donation of his eyes to a blind beggar, and Little Lama's grandfather responds by recommending that we start with small acts that are true to the spirit of compassion.

The drama's appeal, however, is largely limited to the older generation, as is clear from the public performance. Significantly, it is disrupted not only by the drunk young man, but also by Little Lama and his younger brother, who ask the eldest brother (acting on stage) for money to buy tickets for a video screening nearby. This seems to contradict Little Lama's response to the rehearsal, but it is worth remembering that it is the younger brother's idea, and that Little Lama is eager to watch *Journey to the West* (though he ends up watching a Hong Kong action film which is touted as being even better). Still, Little Lama definitely feels the pull of popular culture, and he seems so magnetically attracted to the Monkey King mask that one critic declares that by the end of the film 'the boy no longer seems very fit for the religious life' (Harvey 2006, 34). This needs to be put into perspective by considering the place of *Journey to the West* in *The Silent Holy Stones*.

In the student short, Old Lama is shown to enjoy watching the television dramatisation of the legend, which he heard from his tutor as a novice, and which he told to Little Lama. This suggests a rather smooth, unproblematic transition from traditional oral transmission to the mass media. In the feature, however, the transition is more eventful: one viewing, for instance, is disrupted by a power outage. The viewing experience is also depicted in more detail, and with a greater sense of complexity. During his home visit, Little Lama shows great interest in popular culture, but he also discovers its troubling aspects. He abhors, for instance, the violence in the Hong Kong action film. He is also wary of the way in which the Buddhist monk in *Journey to the West* has become a brand name for a snack. Far from being a cultural dupe, Little Lama is a discerning viewer of the television dramatisation. He particularly identifies with Monkey King, the playful, sometimes mischievous, but always devoted disciple who protects the Buddhist monk from demons and monsters on their way to India to bring Buddhist scriptures to China. It is this image of Monkey King as a faithful disciple and fearless defender that Little Lama sees in the mask. Note that Little Lama never watches the television dramatisation without wearing the mask from the moment that he acquires it, except for on one occasion when he lends it to his double, Little Living Buddha. That is, not until the final episode when the mission of obtaining Buddhist scriptures is accomplished. And this devotion of Monkey King to his master is transferred to Little Lama's close connection to Old Lama. Little Lama is praised by different people on various occasions for his devotion to his master, while the nurturing nature of Old Lama is shown by his insistence on New Year's Eve that, in order to keep his body and mind healthy, Little Lama should not only polish the holy lamps properly (as an act of merit that brings enlightenment), but also should eat well (to avoid being a victim of the ruler of hell). There is a touching moment when Old Lama asks Little Lama to protect him during the planned pilgrimage to Lhasa, just as Monkey King protects the Buddhist monk in *Journey to the West*, and Little Lama answers, putting on the mask, 'As long as Monkey King is here, you have no fear from demons and monsters.'[3]

---

[3] Pema Tseden confirmed that he planned to make a sequel focusing on the pilgrimage to Lhasa, but on a later visit to the village he found the actor who played Little Lama too grown up and no longer suitable for the part; the actor who played Little Lama was in real life a novice, but left the religious order a few years after the film was made.

A strong, close bond forged between a loyal, trusting disciple and an accepting, caring master, drawing inspiration from both the past and the present, suggests that, amid the crisis of traditional Tibetan culture, there is hope. That in the final scene of the film Little Lama arrives at the assembly hall with the Monkey King mask hidden under his robe, almost too late for the religious ritual, need not be considered in a negative light. This is in fact a variation on a motif found in two earlier scenes where, with the mask under his robe, Little Lama offers prayers for the old stone carver, who died shortly after they'd met on his way back home. In the first of these scenes, we are told that the art of stone carving is likely to die out in the area with the old man's departure; inheritance, though incomplete, is suggested when Little Lama (himself the last novice from his village) receives the promised holy stone left unfinished by the old carver. The mood is serene rather than sad when we are shown an empty shot of the colourful prayer flags outside the stone carver's tent, fluttering against a vast sky, with Little Lama heard off-screen chanting a prayer for the departed. In the second scene, the unfinished holy stone is brought back to the quarters of Little Lama and Old Lama, where they offer a prayer for the stone carver before inviting others in the monastery to watch *Journey to the West*. In both scenes, there is no evidence to suggest that the mask under his robe interferes with the integrity of Little Lama as a member of a religious order (in the second scene, it is in fact with the knowledge and approval of Old Lama that Little Lama tucks the mask under his robe). The transfer of the unfinished holy stone across characters and settings in these scenes intimates an act of transmission, a constant movement beyond the immediate context. Thus, the final scene can be considered as a moment in a process of becoming: as the crisp sound of stone carving that opens the film sinks into silence, Little Lama returns to his religious community with the insights gained from his attempts to reach for a connection between tradition and modernity.

The Search

The connection between tradition and modernity, between the spiritual and the mundane, continues to be a subject of inquiry in *The Search* (2007). The film follows a director as he travels with his crew and a business partner in search of actors for a film version of *Drime Kunden*. Drobe, a perfect actress for the female lead, will not play the part without the prince being played by her ex-boyfriend, clearly a ploy to win him back; thus, the crew brings her along to find her ex-boyfriend, who is teaching in a faraway town. As the crew drive in a jeep through landscapes of wide open spaces punctuated by small towns and villages, the businessman tells the story of how he found and lost his first love at the age of eighteen, shortly after he left his religious order. The efforts to find the perfect actors to play Drime Kunden and his wife fail in the end, but prompt important questions about love and compassion in contemporary Tibet.

The Search is a hypertext of *The Silent Holy Stones*. First, the link between life on and off stage is retained, but in a reverse order. In *The Silent Holy Stones*, the older brother and his girlfriend, who play the prince and his wife in the live performance of *Drime Kunden*, are about to marry, which prompts Little Lama to comment that it is only right for the union of the legendary couple to be reflected in real life. In *The Search*, the director aims to use a film-within-a-film technique to bring out the difference between the person and the performer. And the best candidates for the leading roles happen to be lovers who have broken up, rather than individuals who are planning a wedding.

Second, the motif of moving between monastic life and the masses recurs in *The Search*, but the direction is different. Whereas *The Silent Holy Stones* ends with Little Lama returning to the monastery after being exposed to the outside world, the businessman in *The Search* experiences first love shortly after leaving the religious order.

Third, the stories of Drobe, the director and the businessman are set against a background of escalating cultural crisis, signalled at the start when a village boy has to be bribed to run errands, echoing the materialistic mentality of Little Lama's younger brother.

Fourth, the same scene from the legend of *Drime Kunden* is performed, but with entirely different effects. In *The Silent Holy Stones*, the rehearsal scene shows Little Lama paying close attention to the performance, appreciative of its power to inspire and aware that the legend is being transferred to the contemporary context. In *The Search*, the scene is performed by actors auditioned by the director. Here, the prince and his wife are performing in costume, whereas their three children (two are played by the same actors in *The Silent Holy Stones*) are in their school uniforms, each with a red scarf tied around their neck, a sign of their immersion in the official doctrines of the Chinese Communist Party. This creates a strong sense of incongruity reflected in the poor performance of the actors—the children forget their lines, and the prince confesses being distracted by the red scarves. This faltering performance is but one in a series of failures to find an actor for the role of Drime Kunden, which seems to suggest a sense of pessimism: that the compassion of the prince is either irrelevant or impossible.

Thus, with a deepening sense of cultural crisis, a revisitation of *The Silent Holy Stones* prompts reflection about the role of compassion and the possibility of love. In *The Search*, a critical view of compassion is taken by a nightclub singer who used to play Drime Kunden in his home village. He will no longer play the part because he believes that the prince has no right to give away his wife to another man as an act of charity. This appears to be a perfectly reasonable argument, except that it comes from a drunk and quarrelsome man who bullies Drobe and declares that he does not believe in love. A response to this argument is that presented by an old man in a village, whom others call 'Living Drime Kunden', so called because as a young man he gave away his beloved wife to a poor, blind widower who had little chance of remarrying. To the director's question of whether he had the right to do so, the old man answers that he consulted his wife and acted with her approval. To the businessman's question of whether he would give away his eyes to those in need, the old man answers that he would if he could (but he did not know before that it was technically possible). It is worth noting that the old man has a daughter (so he did not give her away as a child), and that, when approached for help, he asks the crew to leave him alone because he lacks the ability and interest to act in a film. This response is admittedly uncommon, but not groundless, as a donation should never be made without dialogue and consensus with those concerned, and true charity comes from the heart. It is also worth noting that, because the shot is taken either from a distance or from the back, we never fully see the face of this old man, suggesting perhaps that compassion is a mystery, one that we never stop pondering.

We also never fully see the face of Drobe, whose lower face is always covered by a scarf that is a gift from her ex-boyfriend. This perhaps suggests that love is also a mystery, one that is explored in the film with a great sense of discovery through interweaving and interrupting stories that involve a variety of characters. This narrative strategy echoes the proliferation of characters who are combinations and permutations of positions in *The Silent Holy Stones*, and becomes more elaborate as Pema Tseden makes a conscious attempt to transfer the traditional art of Tibetan *thangka* painting to film: 'For *The Search*, I have applied the same logic of painting and storytelling employed in a traditional *thangka*, [in which] many stories, like the lives of the Buddha, can be expressed in a single painting' (quoted in Erickson 2013, 70). *The Search* adopts a form of intermediality in which painting is, to use the words of Dick Higgins (2001, 52), 'fused conceptually' with film. In other words, rather than drawing on a particular pictorial event, the film evokes the effect of a *thangka* painting through a juxtaposition that reveals connections. As a result, characters blend into each other. Drobe becomes the characters in the businessman's story when we see her face framed by the side window of the crew's jeep, and hear the voice of the businessman saying off-screen that his story is 'just like a film'. We see tears welling up in her eyes as she attentively follows the growing intimacy between the young ex-monk and his first love in the story. We see her lost in thought as she hears the woman in the story say, 'With you, even begging is a blessing.' The businessman becomes Drobe when he defends her against the nightclub singer by saying, 'That's love.' The director becomes the businessman by taking up the latter's perspective on a pair of lovers lounging in the grass as the crew drive past: 'Love gives you this sense of mystery.' The director and the cameraman become each other every time the camera starts filming. And the driver becomes the director by mentioning the film project in his banter with a young woman who has her lower face covered by a scarf (this is one in a series of women with a scarf over their lower face in *The Search*, and later in the shooting script of *Tharlo*). Consequently, resemblances proliferate. Drobe resembles the young ex-monk's first love, who in turn resembles a young Han Chinese woman in Chengdu. The young ex-monk loses the love of his life to someone who, like Drobe's ex-boyfriend, is a schoolteacher. We are reminded of this schoolteacher, who rides a bike to work, when we see a man and a woman wearing a scarf and riding pillion in front of the jeep.

This proliferation of resemblances takes place even across films, as is clear from the scene where the crew finally find Drobe's ex-boyfriend Kathub Tashi, played by an actor of the same name, who also plays Little Lama's older brother in *The Silent Holy Stones*. In the school staff room, Kathub Tashi gives a short performance that is as moving as the rehearsal in *The Silent Holy Stones*, using a pen as a prop knife to gouge his eyes out for a blind man who needs them. Significantly, Kathub Tashi describes to the director how an acting experience from his college days has enabled him to imagine the pain of unrequited love. This change of perspectives, this expansion of experience, this emancipation from fixed positions, is also evident in Drobe, as she imaginatively identifies with different characters, taking up varying perspectives and critically reflecting on their implications. In fact, the meeting between Drobe and Kathub Tashi involves a constant change of perspectives that invites reflection. A medium shot of Kathub Tashi looking out the window onto the playground (where Drobe is waiting) echoes shots of Drobe looking out the jeep's side window. We are made aware of another perspective as the camera cuts to an over-the-shoulder shot of the cameraman zooming in on Kathub Tashi (whose image is seen on the monitor). The camera continues to place emphasis on different perspectives when a long shot of Drobe standing in the playground, with her back to the camera, looking in the direction of the staff room in the background, cuts to a shot showing Kathub Tashi walking away from the camera to meet Drobe in the background. For about one minute, Drobe and Kathub Tashi are shown as two tiny stationary figures, flanked by students dancing in great circles to loud music from a sound system. Because Drobe and Kathub Tashi are almost motionless, and because their conversation is not heard, we become especially aware of the students' constant turnings, a pattern of movement that continues in the final scene of the film, but in another form.

In the final scene, we learn that the director's wife is recovering from influenza, which is Drobe's pretext for wearing the scarf. Then we see a woman, with a scarf over her lower face, crossing the road from left to right. Shortly afterwards, a lama in his monk's robe crosses the road from right to left. As the jeep takes a turn, Kathub Tashi comes into sight, with Drobe's scarf in hand. We learn that Drobe has no use for the scarf now—she has learnt much from the businessman's story. Kathub Tashi says that seeing her back home has left his heart 'empty' (the same term used by the businessman when he saw off his first love), and that they will play Drime Kunden and his wife for the New Year celebration again, but for the last time. In this pattern of turnings and transformations, characters appear in different guises and move in different directions, suggesting an exploration of possibilities and a critical examination of past and present experiences. Read as a palimpsest, *The Search* revisits *The Silent Holy Stones* to explore ways of understanding love and compassion in a context where Buddhism, along with the traditional Tibetan way of life in which it is embedded, faces challenges of materialism and other forces unleashed by economic development. This revisitation involves a process of transformation that underlines the unfixity of the self and resists narrative closure. The sense of openness is suggested by the fact that in the end the crew never fully see the face of Drobe, a reminder that, like compassion, love is a mystery that must be pondered forever, and that pessimism is perhaps premature.

Old Dog

Old Dog (2010) is a bleak film, especially if read as a hypertext of Pema Tseden's previous films, in particular *The Grassland*.

In *The Grassland*, the theft of a sacred yak is seen as a shocking example of the dissolution of the traditional Tibetan way of life. The material conditions of this cultural crisis are spelt out more clearly in *Old Dog*. Here, the object of theft is a Tibetan mastiff. This rare breed, which figures as a family companion and protector in *The Grassland*, is sold for feverish prices because it has become a commodity coveted by newly rich Han Chinese. In this way, the theft of the mastiff represents a dispossession and commodification of an icon of Tibetan culture by the privileged few profiting from the Chinese Communist Party's drive for economic development, which has spawned boomtowns across China.

In *The Grassland*, the culprit turns out to be Juga, the son of the chieftain Dorlo. A sense of reconciliation and a return to tradition are suggested at the end of the film when father and son set out with a yak to make restitution and seek forgiveness, with the chanting of a Buddhist prayer in the background. A difficult father-son relationship can also be found in *Old Dog*, which opens with the young herdsman Gonpo (Drolma Kyab, who also plays Juga in *The Grassland*) selling a mastiff that his father Akku has kept for thirteen years. Gonpo thinks that it is better to sell it before it is stolen. But the next day Akku takes it back, because a mastiff is 'a herdsman's friend' and not for sale under any circumstances. Whereas

Juga is a horse-riding herdsman, Gonpo is shown riding a motorbike along a road (flanked by barbed-wire fencing) leading to a boom town, there to sell the mastiff to a Han Chinese dealer, or to take his wife to the hospital to investigate their failure to conceive (not her fault, the doctor says). The image of Gonpo riding pillion with his wife, with a scarf over her lower face, is in fact a transformation from two similar images: one in *The Silent Holy Stones* involving Little Lama's older brother and his girlfriend (itself a transformation of the union between Drime Kunden and his wife); the other in *The Search*, suggesting the possibility of love, and later on further transformed into a more complicated relationship in *Tharlo* between the protagonist and his temptress. But infertility is not the only symptom of the crisis of traditional Tibetan culture. In *The Silent Holy Stones* the motorbike and the television set are symbols of status and emerging technologies, whereas in *Old Dog* the television set is associated with crass consumerism, and the motorbike becomes a metaphor for alcoholism when it is left lying on the ground by a drunk Gonpo. Tellingly, Juga is a pipe smoker, whereas Gonpo is unable to enjoy pipe smoking, which is preferred by his father, suggesting the extent to which Gonpo is removed from the tradition. There is a redeeming moment when, after the mastiff is released into a sacred area and then stolen (a situation similar to the theft of the sacred yak in *The Grassland*), Gonpo retrieves it from the Han Chinese dealer, who bought it on the black market. Significantly, this moment is told, not shown; more importantly, this act of resistance costs Gonpo a heavy fine and fifteen days in custody for seriously hurting the dealer.

It is during Gonpo's incarceration that, out in the pasture by the road, watching the eagles gliding overhead, Akku decides to kill the mastiff himself rather than allow it to be stolen. In a desperate act of self-dispossession, Akku strangles the mastiff on the barbed wire fence (a sign of oppression, restriction and violence), so that the mastiff becomes a symbol of the sacrifice and suffering of the Tibetan people. It is a bleak vision of an oppressed people. Whereas *The Grassland* ends with reconciliation and restitution, here we see a father separated from his son, and we hear the sound of a sacred animal being strangled to death. Yet a sense of hope is hinted at when the camera, shooting into the sun, shows visible rays of light reaching the sacrificial victim. Oppression will not be forgotten, as is stressed by Akku's long look at the (off-screen) fallen mastiff. And a desire for freedom and change is suggested by the final shot, a long tracking shot of Akku as he walks away from the fence, climbs a gentle slope and finds open grassland with mountains in the distance and white clouds against a blue sky. In other words, a return to the opening of *The Grassland*, as if steps are retraced when one meets not a running stream, but a barbed wire fence. But this is not a nostalgic return to old certainties, because the opening of *The Grassland*, as noted earlier, initiates a process of transformation that is open to new possibilities. Most importantly, that there is hope amid bleak circumstances is beautifully captured in the penultimate scene with an improvisation that is as spontaneous and unpredictable as life—for more than three minutes, the camera waits patiently as a stray sheep tries again and again to cross the barbed wire fence, breaking free when stuck, backtracking in search of opportunities, until finally it succeeds in finding a gap under the fence.

The Sacred Arrow

The Sacred Arrow (2014) differs from Pema Tseden's other films in terms of both production and reception: it received government funding, and has garnered less international acclaim. The two may in fact be related. Foreign reviews suggest that *The Sacred Arrow* may not be the critics' choice among Pema Tseden's films (Lee 2014, Kerr 2014). This may be attributed to the fact that this government-funded film is not primarily addressed to festival audiences. *The Sacred Arrow* was funded by the government of Jentsa County, Malho Tibetan Autonomous Prefecture[4] of Qinghai Province. According to Pema Tseden, the funder did not impose any constraints on the film's content or his creative approach; the only requirement was that the film should feature archery and be readily accessible to the general public.[5] This explains the more mainstream plot and Hollywood-style storytelling that are uncharacteristic of Pema Tseden's other films.

The Sacred Arrow revolves around an annual archery competition between the neighbouring villages of Damo and Lhalong, a time-honoured tradition intended to promote peace and understanding. Lhalong's best

---

[4] In Chinese *pinyin*: Jianzha County of Huangnan Prefecture.

[5] This is confirmed by Pema Tseden in correspondence with the editors.

archer Dradon, determined to avenge his defeat by Damo's ablest archer Nyima, resorts to the use of a modern mechanical bow to secure victory. Dradon is disqualified for gaining an unfair edge, and he becomes even more antagonistic when he learns that his sister Dekyid and Nyima are secretly engaged. Dradon is then reminded of the art and meaning of archery as an ancient Tibetan tradition by his father, who is a former archery champion. Finally, Dradon is able to resolve his conflict with Nyima when they compete fairly, and achieve a draw in a contest to represent their prefecture in a regional archery tournament. The film ends with Dradon and Nyima helping each other up a slope as they make their way home for a celebration. In this narrative of conflict resolution, recurrent motifs from Pema Tseden's previous works can be identified. The most important one being the confrontation between tradition and modernity, as suggested by Nyima's respect for traditional skills and by Dradon's disdain for them, which creates an uneasy relationship with his father. However, as Dradon's emotional journey to discover the truth of tradition culminates in a traditional celebratory ritual, there is a sense of finality not typical of Pema Tseden. Indeed, if the aim was to achieve wide acceptance through a mainstream plot, an unintended consequence was a simplification of the issues concerning tradition and modernity.

Stylistically, *The Sacred Arrow* also seems highly conventional, using, for example, wide panoramic shots to establish contexts, shot-reverse-shots to guide audience interpretation, close-ups to accentuate the leads' glamour and a sentimental score to suggest a sense of heroism (which may strike some as disproportionate to the depicted events). Judging from such textual features, one may be tempted to describe the film as uninspired. However, contextual considerations reveal new dimensions. It is true that festival screenings have not won *The Sacred Arrow* the level of critical acclaim accorded Pema Tseden's other films, but perhaps film festivals are never meant to be the key channel of communication with target audiences. Investment from the provincial government has meant not only financial support, but also greater access to audiences in Qinghai Province. In 2014 and 2015, the government allowed numerous free-of-charge open-air screenings not only in the provincial capital Xining, but also in townships with predominantly Tibetan populations. Pema Tseden's blog statistics show that more than 10,000 people attended these screenings. The majority of these provincial audiences do not have much experience with alternative cinema. Their expectations for films are largely formed along the lines of entertainment adopting mainstream Hollywood narrative formulae. Pema Tseden's customary auteurish style does not communicate successfully to such audiences. However, as proven by the responses some viewers of the film left on Pema Tseden's blog, adopting the more mainstream narrative style appears to have worked well as a communicative strategy. The film has been successful in drawing the attention of these local audiences to the same issues that he explored in other more experimental works. Read as a palimpsest, *The Sacred Arrow* represents an attempt on the part of Pema Tseden to revisit the same themes as in his previous works by using a more popular, less ambivalent mode of expression that is considered more effective in addressing the intended audiences.

In 2015 Pema Tseden returned to a more experimental mode with *Tharlo*, an adaptation of his 2012 short story of the same name. The auteur's consistent interrogation into issues of identity and modernity is accentuated if *Tharlo* is read as a hypertext of the earlier films and of the short story bearing the same title. However, such a discussion necessitates a detour through his literary works first.

FICTION[6]

Pema Tseden's first film was made in 2002, by which time he had already been established as a published writer. His first short story written in Tibetan, and his first in Chinese, were both published in 1991. As with his films, all of his stories are set in the Tibetan region, and therefore can be read as tales about Tibetan lives; however, they are written in such a way that they also enable an allegorical reading of human conditions in a more general and universal sense. This dual significance running through his stories could be an effect of the linguistic medium functioning as a second-level symbolism, which facilitates in Pema Tseden's stories a tendency for themes and concerns to be sublimated onto an idealist realm, and hence be read as universal allegories.

---

[6]   This introduction only focuses on Pema Tseden's stories written in Chinese, due to the editors' linguistic limitations in Tibetan.

Magical realism of the human psyche: 'Temptation' and 'Snows'[7]

It is interesting to note how Pema Tseden's early stories work within the contemporary literary tradition of 'Tibetan magical realism' established largely by Chinese-language writer Tashi Dawa in the 1980s. This is evident in his semi-fictional work *The Master in Tibet*. The influence of magical realism is most pronounced in this legend of Padmasambhava, the opening sentence of which is an unmistakable allusion to Garcia Marquez's *One Hundred Years of Solitude*,

> Many years later, as he faced the vast wilderness of the snow-covered Tibet, the great Vajrayāna master Padmasambhava was to remember that distant previous life when he was inspired by the Buddhas of the Three Lives to study Dharma zealously and take the grand vow. (2006: 2)

'Temptation' (1997) and 'Snows' (1999) are two other examples. 'Temptation' tells the story of the seven-year-old Jamyan Tenzin, who becomes obsessed with an old Buddhist manuscript he sees in the house of a friend Rigdzin Wangmo. His friend's father will not allow him access, and instead locks it away in a coffer. When Jamyang Tenzin reaches fifteen, Rigdzin Wangmo's father dies. He agrees to marry her so that he can gain access to the manuscript. However, on their wedding night the couple have an argument and she denies him the manuscript. He kills her in a fit of rage and runs off with it. In the middle of the night (the souls of) Rigdzin Wangmo and her father come to him in a dream and lead him to the afterworld. There, an old man reveals to him that he was actually the rightful owner of the manuscript in his previous life, and now he has to go back to the mortal world, and then return to the afterworld in five years. When he wakes, he finds a group of lamas praying by his side, one of them being Rigdzin Wangmo's father. They tell him that he has been recognised as a *tulku*, an enlightened man reincarnated into this world, and he is subsequently taken to live in a temple. The manuscript

---

7   Only a few of Pema Tseden's stories have been translated into European languages. The editors have taken care to conform to the titles of existing published translations. The titles of those without existing translations have been translated by the editors.

is presented to him, but placed near a Buddha statue in a high place. He is told that he will be allowed to possess it when he reaches twenty years of age. He continues to pine for it, and watches from a distance every day. Finally, his twentieth birthday comes, but when the lamas bring the manuscript to him, they find him dead in his bedroom. They open the manuscript and lay it on his chest. He feels like he is floating on air with the sense of joy that comes from having the manuscript pressed close to his body. At the end of the ritual that marks the forty-ninth day of his death, his body and the manuscript are cremated together. A young lama, distracted during prayer, opens his eyes and catches sight of him flying into the heavens holding the manuscript in his hands.

The story is predicated on the Tibetan monastic system and the religious belief in reincarnation. Yet, it sets itself apart from many contemporary Chinese representations of Tibet, especially those that adopt magical realism as a narrative structure and focus on the exotic details of Tibetan religion and culture. In 'Temptation' Tibetan culture forms the canvas of the story's focus: Jamyang Tenzin's intense desire for the manuscript. There are scarcely any details of the monastic life in the story, and it offers little room for an ethnographic reading. An exposition of religious beliefs is altogether absent. A cultural reading is equally limiting. Instead, the narrative centres on Jamyang Tenzin's obsession and desire, and abundant descriptions are given concerning his state of mind. For example, the first time that he sees the manuscript:

> At first, Jamyang Tenzin was bewildered. He stood there dumbfounded. His eyes sparkled with a strange light. Neither the little girl nor her father took notice of his state. Suddenly, he felt as if someone was giving him a forceful push and he dashed towards the manuscript. He clutched it to his chest and darted for the door. In that split second, the little girl's father opened his eyes, grabbed him by the calves and pulled him back. He fell flat on the ground and dropped the manuscript. It landed a few steps in front of his face, still shining with a golden light. He neither cried out nor felt any pain, but continued toward the manuscript, struggling to get near it.[8] (2011, 1)

---

[8] All translations here are provided by the editors.

Two points about the narrative are noteworthy. First, there are no specific reasons given for Jamyang Tenzin's fascination with the manuscript. The fact that it belonged to him in his previous life provides no justification for his obsession, except for the concept of ownership as the basis for relationships. This lays bare the nature of human desire. Second, whether he is the rightful owner or not, the object of desire is always beyond the reach of the desiring subject. It is only when one's mortal life ends, and the desire for and awareness of the desired object unite in non-existence, that any joy can be felt. Although the story is set in a Tibetan Buddhist context, its themes of desire, possession and the simultaneous dissipation of life and desire are universal concerns in all literatures.

'Snows' is written in both a Tibetan and Chinese version.[9] A shepherd finds a baby girl with a translucent body in the snow after dreaming about his wife running across a snow-covered landscape. He names the girl Snow and nurtures her as she grows into a beautiful and healthy child. When Snow grows up, she meets a young boy who looks exactly like her and is also named Snow. He also has a translucent body and was found by his mother in the snow after she had a dream. The two develop a bond, and when their parents meet, they recognise one another as the spouse in each other's dream. They live happily together until a drought strikes the grassland. The boy Snow decides to show his body for cash in order to feed the village. Yet, when tourists, researchers and reporters hear about his sister, they offer money to see her body as well. When their demands are rejected, they bribe the villagers into kidnapping the brother and sister in order to satisfy their curiosity. On the night of the planned kidnapping, the entire village have the same dream: an old man tells them the two Snows are spirits of the snow mountain, and they are not to harm them. The shepherd and his wife also dream of the same old man; he tells them he is taking the spirits back to snow mountain. When they wake in the morning, they can no longer find the two Snows.

Readers who are familiar with Pema Tseden's Tibetan background and his films might interpret this story as a parable of contemporary Tibet's socio-political situation, or read it as a story about the exploitation of the Tibetan environment and community by outsiders. This is definitely one

---

[9]   This analysis is based on the Chinese version of the story and an English translation of the Tibetan version, kindly provided by Pema Tseden.

possible interpretation, but if this is the only intention of the text, the first part of the story about the good shepherd's compassion and care for the two Snows, and the elaborations on their goodness would be redundant. The two Snows are unfailingly trusting, generous and magnanimous. Their deeds are never motivated by considerations of grandiose heroism. The contrast between compassion and greed, as emphasised in the narrative, allows the story a second layer of significance: the more idealist exploration of innocence itself. It grows into something beautiful when benevolently nurtured, but can only retreat, or even dissipate, when met with evil intentions. The story's mythical plot and characterisation eschews descriptions of mundane details necessary for realistic stories, and enables a sublimation of the theme of innocence on a more conceptual level.

Anti-ethnography: 'Ogyen's Teeth'

'Ogyen's Teeth' (2011) is one of Pema Tseden's best-known stories, one which does not only resist a restrictive local reading of Tibetan relevance, but also subverts the common stereotyping and the ethnographic approach to Tibet in Chinese and Western texts. This is representative of his later stories and all of his films that exhibit the same acute awareness of the danger of ethnographic essentialism. On a rare occasion when he was speaking about his literary works rather than his films, he recalled consciously restraining himself and avoiding stereotypical treatment of reincarnation in the story. He made certain that the focus was placed on the character's 'human aspect'.[10]

Ogyen was the narrator's old classmate. He remembers the former not being exactly the brightest student in class. He often let him copy his homework and exams to help him out. Unlike the narrator, Ogyen did not make it to the city for tertiary education and left school early. Soon after the narrator moved to the city to study, he was told that Ogyen had been identified as a reincarnated *tulku*. Then, visiting home over a holiday, his mother urged him to visit *Tulku* Ogyen so as to ask for

---

[10] 'Pema Tseden on Literature and Locale'. At Hong Kong Baptist University, 30th October 2015. His full speech is available at https://www.youtube.com/watch?v=DkVmfcxkzM4.

his blessing. The narrator was initially unhappy about the disparity in their relative status, but they quickly became friends again. The story's narrative present takes place after the narrator hears about Ogyen's death. The monastery has decided to build a memorial stupa for him, and asks his father for the *tulku's* primary teeth. His father presents to the monastery everything he has, including teeth he has collected from their roof. They are all purported to be Ogyen's primary teeth, some of which had been tossed up on the roof when he was a child. However, the total number of teeth is now fifty-eight, and because there is no way to differentiate the *tulku's* teeth, the monastery decides to place all fifty-eight into the stupa. At this point the narrator remembers that once when they were playing in Ogyen's house as children, he had lost a tooth, which Ogyen's father proceeded to toss onto the roof for him. That tooth is now resting in the stupa, receiving the public's displays of piety and respect.

In the magically realistic 'Temptation' and 'Snows' human desire and human goodness are both sublimated to a magnitude larger than life, nearly reaching the level of magnificence. Desire and goodness manifest themselves in their most essential form. However, 'Ogyen's Teeth' works in the opposite direction. The dignified *tulku* starts out as a simple boy. Among the presumed awe-inspiring relics is a tooth from the narrator. It has made its way into the stupa in an utterly inconsequential manner. What is supposed to be sanctified is in fact commonplace. Instead of the sublimation of the mundane, this story ends in a humorous bathos. The fall from grace is achieved by deflating the grandiose image of Ogyen, showing him as obtuse, a fact well known by the narrator, and interjecting Ogyen's story with reference to the mundane paths taken by the narrator. Conspicuous by their absence are stereotypical descriptions of the Tibetan landscape, or references to mystical Tibetan spirituality, as expected in mainstream Chinese writing about Tibet. This piece is particularly important among Pema Tseden's short stories, as it displays the author's acute awareness of the Tibetan stereotype in circulation, and by extension the potential danger of Tibetan film and fiction being straitjacketed by the signifying ghetto of ethnographic, or immediate political relevance.

From pastoral isolation to urban utilitarianism: 'Eight Sheep', 'Artists', 'Holy Stones, Quietly Chiseled'

Audiences of Pema Tseden's films would find the same concern about the impacts of modernity on Tibetan lives in the auteur's later short stories. After all, it is an issue that has been central in Tibetan society, and thus in the social background that underpins all his works. 'Eight Sheep' (2009) deals with the pastoral population's encounter with outsiders. The shepherd boy Gyalo is sad as he mourns his deceased mother. He is still wearing the coat his mother made for him although the weather has now turned warm. One day as he is tending his sheep on the grasslands, he comes upon a foreigner. They speak to each other in their respective languages without understanding one another. As the foreigner leaves, 'a fear suddenly dawns on Gyalo. At this moment, he hears the bleating of his sheep echoing behind him.' (2011, 168) A layered reading of this story is possible. On one level the ending shows the difficulty of communication between people who speak different languages. Language is taken not only literally but also metaphorically to refer to discourses that people subscribe to and speak in. A feeling of isolation strikes the young shepherd after his failure to communicate with another human being. This induces a nearly existential angst, and the story certainly affords the interpretation of such a universal theme. However, if the figure of the deceased mother is read as a metaphor for a lost mother culture, the more specific relevance to contemporary Tibet cannot be overlooked. The clearly designated identity of the intruder being a *laowai* (foreigner, stranger) creates a divide between the young shepherd and the stranger. This particular divide is specific to a rustic, isolated existence and a foreign consciousness that signifies modernity. The shepherd's fear is induced by an encounter with the unknown and the anticipation of imminent major changes brought about by further intrusion. He is facing the same changes as all the other characters in Pema Tseden's films and stories. Consistent with his earlier stories, which pay more attention to the depiction of human psychology, and in contrast to the critical realism focusing on Tibet in his films, the existentialist anguish of the individual facing such a situation is the centre of attention of this tale.

'Artists'[11] (2014) is a story about an old lama in the company of a novice on a pilgrimage to Lhasa when they come across some Chinese-speaking (ethnicity unspecified) philistines who are posing as 'artists'. They praise the old lama's full-body prostrations as brilliant acts of performance art. They then invite him to contribute to a 'work of art' by writing the six-syllable mantra on the thousands of *khata*-scarves they are transporting. On those *khatas* they also will invite Chinese students they meet along the way to write in Chinese 'I love Beijing Tian'anmen'. For doing this the lama will be paid one *yuan* for each *khata*. The *khatas* will then be tied together to form a connection from Beijing to Lhasa. The old lama does not agree and the 'artists' leave. At the end of the story the lama sees a plane flying in the direction of Lhasa. The novice tells his master that it only takes a few hours to reach Lhasa by plane, which the latter considers to be much too fast. The attitude of the philistines towards the religious act of pilgrimage borders on the profane, and their behaviour toward the Tibetan cultural icon of the *khata* borders on vandalism. The old lama disapproves of them and regrets the speed of the plane, as he cherishes the spiritual process of the pilgrimage. Yet, there is nothing he can do to rectify these anomalies, nor does he show any intention of doing so. Like Gyalo in 'Eight Sheep', the lamas in 'Artists' have just experienced their first encounters with people from the outside world. The dramatic irony is contained in the knowledge of the readers but not of the characters—that these first encounters will be followed by a more intense confrontation of the two worlds. These seemingly inconsequential encounters are indeed part of a much more far-reaching intrusion of the outside world that will eventually exacerbate and alienate these characters from a life they can comprehend. 'Artists' and 'Eight Sheep' capture the state of mind of the individuals during their first encounters with an unknown at a time when they are yet to realise that this unknown will change their lives beyond recognition.

In 'Holy Stones, Quietly Chiseled' (2014), the rupture of tradition is explored from yet another perspective. Lobsang regrets his recklessness, as he is not by his mother's side when she dies, because he is out getting

---

[11] Pema Tseden confirmed that this story forms a film script that was intended to be the sequel to *The Silent Holy Stones*. After that plan was scrapped, he published the treatment as a short story in 2014 in *Guangming Daily*. It was finally reprinted in a 2016 collection.

drunk. Later on, she comes to him in a dream and asks him to have a holy stone carved for her. This turns out to be a problem as the dream transpires only a few days after the sole remaining stone carver who knows how to craft holy stones has died. On another night he is again drunk and passing by where the old stone carver used to work. No one is around, but he can hear the sound of a chisel on stone. He is puzzled, but does not think more about it until the old stone carver appears to him in a dream. He tells him that his deceased mother has asked for the holy stone that he promised her husband years ago. From this point on, Lobsang goes to the same place every day to leave butter tea for the old stone carver's spirit, and every day he sees that progress has been made on the stone. After the stone is finished, he brings it to the local monastery for blessing. The lamas entrust him with the task of asking for another carved stone from the old stone carver's spirit, since he is the only person who can communicate with the latter. The stone carver's spirit denies this request, because he is too tired to carve another. Lobsang discusses this with his deceased mother in a dream, and they decide to offer their stone to the monastery as a gift. The similarity in the title of this story to *The Silent Holy Stones* prompts an associative reading of the two works.[12] To follow on from the palimpsestic reading of *The Grassland* and *The Silent Holy Stones*, the figure of the old stone carver's spirit in this story needs to be read as one and the same character as the stone carver Zoba in *The Grassland* and the stone carver who dies at the end of *The Silent Holy Stones*. His death finally marks the end of the tradition in that area. Even as a spirit he is too tired to carve another stone. The life force of this tradition is definitively exhausted. This critical focus on the difficulty for traditional ways of life to endure in the contemporary world is pronounced. In addition, there is a secondary focus: it is only when Lobsang is drunk[13] or dreaming that he is able to communicate with the spirits of his mother and the stone carver. Perhaps it is the individual's

---

[12] Pema Tseden has indicated to the editors that the story was originally commissioned as a 'cinema novella' of *The Silent Holy Stones* following the success of the film. He started writing the piece in that direction but his ideas changed course during the writing to arrive at its present form.

[13] Elsewhere Pema Tseden has displayed a more critical attitude to the drinking problem of young Tibetan men. One example is the scene in which young people drink with abandon in the woods after their village is defeated in an archery competition in *The Sacred Arrow*.

affiliation with the Tibetan collective subconscious that allows their culture and distinctive identity to survive. The states of dreaming and intoxication symbolise the retrieval of such a collective subconscious. Therefore, tradition is not dead, only dormant. When it is impossible for the tradition that people value to continue in everyday life, it resides like a buried treasure beneath the surface of reality. This story provides hope in the form of a collective subconscious. It resorts to a more general human experience of history in order to conceive alternatives to utter hopelessness in the immediate context of Tibet.

Faux naïf, rondo, and folklore

One consistent characteristic in Pema Tseden's short stories is the apparent simplicity of his protagonists. They are always simple folk such as shepherds, rural women, novices, labourers or unemployed young men. They survive at the bottom of the food chain in a modern urban world. Their apparent passivity, like femininity to Simone de Beauvoir, is a condition, not a nature. They are not scribes of the dominant discourses in their world. In the stories, they are quiet and reticent. They have an ingenuous demeanour, are straight with people and spare in both speech and expression. They are always presented in an attentive rather than a distracted mode. Most description of them tends to be focused on the single action or situation in which they are engaged. The portrayal of their psychological and emotional modulations is often restricted to the shortest possible account of a facial expression in a brief sentence. This easily leads to the superficial interpretation of these characters being simple and naïve, seemingly incapable of complicated psychological and intellectual processes. In fact, there is another way to understand such an extremely restrained characterisation. A comparably restrained 'emotion-scape' is present in musical chants. In chants the intervals of the musical notes are often narrow and repetitive. Many chants used in religious occasions might sound monotonous, but they always carry highly impassioned religious sentiments. It is this discrepancy between the magnitude of the passion conveyed in the lyrics and the unruffled and monotonous expression of the melody that creates the tension, which is more powerful than any sensational expressions can produce. The plight of the underdog—being deprived and muted, only surviving whatever comes its way—is precisely what is being explored and exposed in

Pema Tseden's stories. The naivety of his characters is only the *faux naïf*. It is a powerful expression of ordinary people helplessly facing the impersonal turmoil of *progress*, as described by Walter Benjamin (1992, 249), in the relentless pursuit of *development* in contemporary Tibet under Chinese policies.

In addition to characterisation, the same sense of the *faux naïf* permeates all of Pema Tseden's fictional narratives maintained by a formal minimalism. Traditionally, critics of Realist fiction value the construction of life-like worlds in the narrative universe. A narrative replete with meticulous and imaginative details of the characters' circumstances—such as their physical environments or their psychological and mental activities—is generally considered to be a sign of a good novel. Obvious examples of this are Dickens' novels and the Chinese classic *Dream of the Red Mansion*. The characters in these fictional masterpieces are constructed with copious details of their situations, their engagements with people, their material realities and the events happening around them. Readers view them as multi-faceted social beings. However, this is not the case in Pema Tseden's stories. Instead, a minimalist tenor is always adopted for the narrative voice. There is a remarkable absence of contrived nomenclature and complex syntax. The drama of the stories is established with imaginative plots rather than manufactured suspense. The narration is stripped of any artifice, and evades all elaborations, other than required information about the protagonists' situations and actions. They show a measured management of affect expressed in an extremely focused style. This lays bare the essential state of the characters and their circumstances and the very notions that the stories intend to convey. Readers are invited to perceive specific human situations and his characters' responses in their most honest and elemental state. If Pema Tseden's films are a contextualisation of the issues of identity, oppression and change in the situation of Tibet, his stories decontextualise the Tibetan people's situations, so that their plight can inspire a more universal perspective on human sufferings.

A good example is his earlier work 'Where the Moon Rises'[14] (2003), which is a particularly important tale to read if one is to understand

---

[14] An English translation of the complete story is published in the 34-35, 2007 issue of *Voice and Verse*.

the universality of Pema Tseden's stories. As it is the shortest of all his stories and deceptively simple, it often escapes the attention of critics and readers. The tale is only about 3,000 Chinese characters in length and conceived as a myth. A male and a female character, Dawa Tserang and Dawa Drolma, both presented as being extremely child-like, sit under a crimson moon. They have heard in a folk song that in the past the moon was white, and that in the future it will be black. They confirm this with a hermit in a cave who bemoans mankind's greed. He tells them that they will see a white moon if they go towards where it rises, and a black moon where it sets. They decide to find out for themselves, so Dawa Drolma goes towards where the moon rises. There she sees a white moon casting its light on a green pasture, turning it silver. Dawa Tserang goes towards where the moon sets and sees a black moon hanging over a cracked, barren land. After confirming the words of the hermit, they return to meet and report what each has seen. They decide to leave for the pasture on which the white moon shines. This miniature tale recasts the recurrent motif of traditional culture being threatened by a less than ideal future. The succinct treatment of the theme turns this idea into a single focused image, stripped of all realistic contexts and settings. Moreover, for a second time, the archetypal innocent twin-like brother and sister feature in a Pema Tseden story, the other one being 'Snows'. It is not difficult to associate them with the primordial archetype of the brother and sister surviving inside a gourd in the common myth of the great flood that circulates in many cultures. Surely, one can interpret this tale at the level of the universality of cultural change. Although such pessimism about the future is specific to the context of this particular tale, the relevance of contemporary Tibet functions more as a condition of the plot and the theme than an issue in focus to be explored.

Stylistically, it is impossible to overlook the frequent repetitions in 'Where the Moon Rises'. Basically, if the same expression or phrase can be used, it tends to be used repeatedly within a single paragraph. A simple type-token ratio check would reveal that lexical repetition is a general textual feature of Pema Tseden's stories. The opening paragraph of this particular one is a good illustration of this:

The moon has risen.

The *crimson* moon has risen from the mountains in the east, casting *crimson* moonlight across the barren, open country.

Dawa Tserang and Dawa Drolma are sitting side by side. They are gazing at the boundless country washed by the *crimson* moonlight. At the limits of visibility is an expanse of barrenness. Not even a single flower grows there. Nothing but a lifeless silence prevails. (2011, 55, emphasis added)

Such lexical repetition creates an unusual quality of density in the text. Due to the recurrence of these lexical items, they become stylistically marked, and provide an anchor for readers' attention to generate a calming, even meditative, state of mind in the readers to promote a mode of concentrated—rather than distracted or superficial—reading to match the mythic archetypal ambience, and hence the intended universal relevance, of the text.

Repetition in some of Pema Tseden's stories also assumes a structural importance that performs a crucial function. On the one hand, it heightens the meditative quality of the texts, and on another it magnifies the drama of the plot to reinforce the effects of the texts. 'Her Ninth Man'[15] (2012) is structured entirely around repetition. The first half of the story is based on Yongtso recounting to her ninth man her previous eight relationships. None of these relationships share any similarity except that each of the men has exploited her in some fashion. Her first man left the religious life for her, but abandoned her at the end, because he could not stand people's disdain. Her second man abandoned her when his previous woman returned. The third was a jewellery trader from whom she received a necklace with 30 pieces of precious coral, at the price of her body for 30 nights. The fourth was a truck driver who drove her to the city, again, for a price. The fifth was a swindler who took advantage of her and stole her necklace. She was left penniless and walked all the way back to her village. Just at the point of collapse, a shepherd rescued her. He immediately grew to adore her, but his excessive need for sex soon became unbearable. She found help from a local thug to get rid of the sixth and the local thug became her seventh. The thug turned out to be impotent and abusive and Yongtso only managed to leave him by threatening to reveal his impotence to the village. Next she married into a family where the son was the sole descendent. Their only interest was

---

[15] An English translation of the story in full is published in the March 2017 issue of *Cha: An Asian Literary Journal.*

for her to give them an offspring. When her baby died only a few days after birth, she once again left. The narrative is characterised by a similar pattern of disappointment and separation, punctuated with a structurally identical treatment. The following extract comes from the closing section of her account to her ninth man about her first relationship:

> This was Yongtso's story of her first man. She told him all about it. He was her ninth. She withheld nothing from him. This ninth man of hers smiled and said, 'This is the delight between men and women. One simply can't fight it. And it is what has led me to you.'

> Words like these could no longer move her. Her face stayed expressionless. (2014, 72)

After the account of her second man, there is a recapitulation:

> This was Yongtso's story of her second man. She told her ninth man all about it. She did not withhold anything. Her story made him angry, and he said, 'That was wicked of him!' She heard what he said and glanced at him. (73)

Likewise, after the story about her third man:

> This was Yongtso's story about the third man of hers. She told her ninth man all about it, leaving out nothing. This ninth man of hers scoffed and said, 'There are no decent traders in the world. They are all deceitful and greedy.'

> At hearing this, she looked at him again. (75)

As her ninth man repeatedly expresses sympathy to Yongtso about her previous experience, both she and the readers become gradually convinced of the possibility of a happy ending. However, this anticipation is soon negated. After Yongtso marries her ninth man, he starts drinking with his friends once a month. Each time he returns home drunk, he makes denigrating remarks to Yongtso about one of her previous relationships. After eight such incidents in eight months, she leaves him. In the morning he wakes to find that she has cut off and left her two plaits of hair by his bedside. The text succeeds in creating a sense of surprise through the repetition being resumed rather than disrupted, as is anticipated. The reader's anticipation of a happy ending is thwarted; the reader's frustration mirrors and accentuates that of the protagonist.

'Phurbu' (2015)[16] is another of Pema Tseden's stories in which the thematic focus is subtly honed by a thoughtful use of repetition. Phurbu is a day-labourer in this eponymous tale set in the 1930s. He is a simple man. He has an unusually large appetite and eats three times the amount of a normal person at every meal. He is conscientious and works remarkably hard. He travels around with his donkey searching for work. On those occasions when there is no work to be found, and the pair are on the brink of starvation, he sells off the donkey which always finds its way back to him. As the story begins, they are followed by a hungry wolf that attempts to attack them at night, although he has taken care to leave food behind for it. Angered by its ingratitude, he kills it with a single blow from his staff. Then Phurbu and his donkey find work on a plantation. One day, Phurbu and his companions get into a fight with labourers from a rival plantation. The labourers come at night to burn down their crops in revenge. Phurbu's supervisor can no longer afford to keep him, and while casting him away he hurls abuse. Phurbu feels particularly hurt because his loyalty is not being appreciated. In an uncontrollable rage he strikes him with his staff and accidentally kills him. Phurbu buries him and leaves. He next meets a widow and her daughter. He stays with them until frost kills her crops and she can no longer afford to keep him around. She asks him to leave but he refuses. She tries to poison him but he finds out and kills her. He packs up whatever he can take away, including the widow's daughter and the donkey. Out on the road they soon meet a caravan, the chief of which takes them in. By accident, not intention, Phurbu is used by bandits to rob the caravan and kill nearly everyone. Phurbu is mistaken as an accessory to the crime and is jailed. When he is released years later from prison, his homeland is already part

---

[16] In a 2015 interview Pema Tseden revealed that the story was intended as a film script about a Tibetan serf that was commissioned by another director. He finished writing the script but it was shelved because the serf he depicted 'was too free and did not match the image that the production unit had of serfs.' Access to the full interview at https://www.youtube.com/watch?v=ELxqD8ucO1w.

of the People's Republic and a new ethos has set in. On the day of his release, the widow's daughter and donkey come to meet him. They take him to the land that has been given to them by the new government, but Phurbu does not trust it; he is unable to accept any sense of permanent stability. After the donkey dies, he tells the young woman that he was her mother's murderer, a truth that she already knows. Then he leaves.

There is a recurrent pattern in Phurbu's experience: trusting his patron— feeling betrayed—killing his patron as an act of nullifying his initial trust. This repetitive pattern is accentuated by all three of his patrons repeating to him in jest, 'Eat all you can, then work with all your vigour.' All three are killed by a single blow of his staff. His last patron, that is, the new government that has given them the land to work, is different and their relationship does not follow the same pattern of trust— betrayal—destruction. However, the story's readers know that after the initial years of land reform, political campaigns were launched and many individuals were harmed and killed. Phurbu's scepticism about the livelihood provided by the new government is based on wisdom gained from experience, which is ultimately what sets him on the road again. The story ends at this point. What happens after this 'optimistic' period is well known to Pema Tseden's readers, thus rendering the optimism of that period ironic. The absence of his disillusionment with 'liberation' in the story does not conceal the fact of its reality. On the contrary, this creates a deafening silence that only accentuates it. This effect is achieved by the abrupt interruption of the repetitive pattern.

In an interview about his literary works, Pema Tseden acknowledged his conscious use of repetition as a rhetorical device, and attributed this to his study of Indian poetics as part of his formal education in Tibetan language and literature.[17] Another apt analogy of the structural repetition in his stories would be the musical structure of a rondo. The rondo is a song structure commonly found in European folk songs. Episodes, or digressions, are planted between the refrains. Embellishments and adjustments are accommodated in the refrains to provide variation. The refrain provides an anchorage point for the reader's attention, reinforcement of empathy, and anticipation of events in the coming verse. Each time Phurbu finds a new patron, readers anticipate

---

[17] Full interview accessed at https://www.youtube.com/watch?v=ELxqD8ucO1w.

betrayal and destruction. As soon as Yongtso begins to recount one of her relationships, readers instantly feel sorry for her, as they begin to anticipate another moment of exploitation and disappointment. The accumulated events—and the repeated anticipation and fulfillment of the anticipation—serve to magnify the effect of the events. As with a piece of music, such texts create a rhythm in the readers' consciousness; their affective dimension impinges on the readers' psychological response, which may last even after the memory of the narrative has faded.

As with folk songs, repetition is also routinely employed in folk narratives. Vladimir Propp and William Labov, among many linguists and narratologists, have highlighted the importance of recursive narrative structures. Labov and others have identified repetition as a narrative strategy that achieves a wide range of purposes, including the promotion of narrative credibility. Propp has also identified the recursive narrative structure as being a major component in his morphology of folklore (1968). Such extensive use of structural repetition in music and folklore can be explained by the oral nature of both. There are many other corpora of early writing that demonstrate similar strategies. Many of these have been passed down orally and then only later were written down. Repetition has remained in the written form of many folkloric tales, myths and legends. Such texts record memories of early human situations such as the great flood and other archetypal foundational narratives related to early humans' experience of survival and of nature. As a result, repetition has acquired an association with these archetypal narrations. Through the intense employment of repetition and a consistent fostering of the *faux naïf*, Pema Tseden's tales acquire an ethos that evokes early archetypal folklores. Such an effect intensifies the universality of the tales and extends the relevance of the Tibetan experience.

FILM AND FICTION

It is fascinating then to look at Pema Tseden's two distinct bodies of creative work, namely his films and his fiction, in a comparative light. The two carry the structure of feeling, to borrow Raymond Williams' notion, of the same creative subject (1993, 18). They reflect the lived experience of the creative subject's time and locale, and his understanding and reflection of his milieu. Yet, the two forms are imbued with the histories of their respective conventions, and are enabled and constrained by their respective modalities of expression.

In both his films and fiction, Pema Tseden creates artistic images of individuals facing changes within their environment. These changes include the fading traditional rustic life of the Tibetan grasslands, where religious values were originally able to provide an anchor for community life, and the incursion of a consumerist and utilitarian urban culture in which nothing is sacred and all values are fleeting. Whether Pema Tseden's characters intend to willingly embrace or reluctantly refuse these changes is irrelevant. It is a fact of life they are faced with, so they are shown to be simply journeying on their paths in life, and living through these changes in whichever way they can. Each of Pema Tseden's characters struggles to find his/her co-ordinates in a world s/he is trying to catch up with. Ama Tsomo in *The Grassland* is reluctant to deal with the theft. She does not approve of the village chieftain's insistence on punishment, based on his modern administrative sense of justice, because she believes it runs contrary to her compassionate intention of setting free the yak in the first place. The old lama in 'Artists' is unimpressed with the profane attitude toward pilgrimage and prayer embodied in the trendy Chinese-speaking crowd. Finding oneself in the situation of negotiating a position amidst change is a common concern in all of Pema Tseden's works. Yet, there is a divergence in the functions of these human stories told in the cinematic and the literary forms, and this divergence is made possible by the creative subject's acute awareness of the predisposition of their respective modalities of expression. His films necessarily provide concrete visual images of Tibet, and thus generate realistic references, thereby guiding reception and interpretation in a realistic mode. Literature, on the contrary, resides entirely in the readers' imagination, and is therefore less constricted by realistic references and more open to allegorical interpretation. A comparison of Pema Tseden's two bodies of work shows that the issues of Tibet's socio-political situation and Tibetan identity feature more prominently in his films, while the universality of the characters' situations in relation to general human conditions surfaces more effectively in the short stories. These two bodies of work show a keen awareness of the potentiality inherent in the two forms. For example, the fluid nature of identity explored in *The Search* would be extremely difficult, if indeed at all possible, to be represented entirely by linguistic means in a short story. Likewise, the rhythmic construction of anticipation and disillusionment in 'Her Ninth Man' would not only be ineffective in a film, but also would appear forced and tedious.

It is in this respect that the importance of the film *Tharlo* can be assessed. It is the first of Pema Tseden's films in which contemporary Tibetan relevance and the more universal allegorical function have seamlessly merged in the cinematic representation of the story.

THARLO

Pema Tseden's audience would agree that *Tharlo* represents the highest artistic achievement of the auteur's creativity so far. Its symbolism is notably more comprehensive, consistent and focused than in any of his previous works. Its finesse in both conception and execution has brought the film-world of Pema Tseden's Tibet into the most emblematic realm of film as moving images that explore life beyond its appearance.

The short story

Tharlo (2012) is the main character of the eponymous short story. He is a guileless shepherd with a ponytail who lives alone in the mountains. At the beginning of the story he goes to the village police station to apply for an identity card, as everyone in the village is told to do so. He reports to the policeman that he does not use his name Tharlo very often because everyone just calls him Ponytail. The policeman tells him he can work out who he is just by looking at him. Tharlo is amazed at this ability of the policeman:

> Tharlo was surprised. He looked at the police chief and asked, 'How did you know?'
>
> The policeman smiled and said, 'We policemen naturally know more than other people.'
>
> With a touch of admiration Tharlo responded, 'No wonder you've been able to catch some of the bad people.' (2014, 151)

The policeman notes that this comment about them catching *some* of the bad people can also be understood as a remark about them not catching *all* of the bad people, but this remark is made on Tharlo's part more as a factual observation, even a commendation, concurring with the policeman's boasting, rather than a put-down. Tharlo's straightforward candour constitutes the mischievous humour of the situation; more noteworthy is the thematic importance of Tharlo's attitude. He is factual, impartial and non-judgemental about the world around him. He has a remarkable capacity for taking in whatever comes his way. He remembers details such as the precise number of ewes and rams he tends, or how many lambs will be born in the coming season. He can recite Mao's speech 'Serve the People' in its entirety, and gives sincere consideration to what is said about good and bad people in the speech. These details show two things. First, Tharlo belongs to the generation who grew up during the Cultural Revolution. Second, they reveal that Tharlo does not forget, therefore symbolically carrying the collective past with him, but ironically, being an orphan, he does not know his own date of birth. He remembers every word learnt during the Cultural Revolution, but does not know anything about himself or his origin. He is an honest shepherd living alone in the mountains. He is content that he is a good person. He is straightforward in his approach to the world. The way he looks at the world is exact and unambiguous. To him the difference between good people and bad people is categorical. His simple life in the mountains has fostered in him a concentrated state of mind without the distraction of other people, purposes and intentions.

However, a trip to the township changes everything. He is told by the local police to go to a photo studio in the township to take a photo, as he needs it to have his identity card issued. As soon as he leaves his isolated environment, he seems out of place. His approach to people and things is viewed in stark contrast with the people he meets in the township, one of them being a hairdresser who seduces him and eventually takes advantage of him. In their first encounter in the barbershop his truthful temperament is contrasted with her insincere nature:

> Tharlo said, 'I herd sheep. I don't have all that much water to wash my hair.'
>
> She put on a deliberate look of surprise, 'Oh, really? Well then, how many sheep do you have?'

Tharlo said without a second thought, 'I have three hundred and seventy-five in total, of them one hundred thirty-three are rams, one hundred and sixty-eight ewes . . .' (160)

The credulous Tharlo is taken in by her 'deliberate look of surprise', not realising the danger of revealing one's own particulars to a stranger 'without a second thought', even in an apparently harmless, casual and idle chat. Indeed, this seemingly inconsequential conversation is to bring serious repercussions. Likewise, Tharlo's encounter with a group of university students near the barbershop also shows a similar contrast between his down-to-earth honesty and their affected pretense:

'We are university students from the Mainland. We are here on holiday. You look unusual. Are you an artist?'

Tharlo was puzzled. He kept smoking and staring at the young student. He had no idea what he was talking about. His facial expression remained very serious.

Another spoke, 'Look at his eyes. They are so deep. He must be an artist of great depth.'

Tharlo paid no attention. He finished his cigarette and chucked the butt on the floor. Then he stamped on it to put it out. 'Actually, I herd sheep.'

Another one spoke, 'Listen to him! He is so deep. He is definitely an artist.' (162)

That night the hairdresser takes him to a karaoke bar. In the morning he wakes up next to her. She asks him to sell his sheep and take her to Lhasa. He refuses because more than half of the sheep that he is hired to herd are not his own. When he returns to the village he blurts out to the policeman that he might have met a bad person, but he does not go into detail and the policeman takes no heed of what he is saying. However, one month later Tharlo brings to the hairdresser the money he has received for selling the sheep. She is, of course, delighted, and as she washes his hair, she convinces him to let her cut off his ponytail so that they will be less conspicuous when they run away. At night they go drinking again. In the morning he wakes up to find that she has disappeared with the money. At the end of the story, Tharlo goes back to the village and tells the policeman he is now a bad person. Still not paying attention to the change he has undergone, the policeman only notices that his ponytail is gone and sends him back for another photograph, since, without the ponytail, the photo on his new identity card no longer resembles him. This is a tale of an individual losing a clear sense of his position in the world, which ironically occurs in the process of institutionalising his identity in the form of an identity card. This short story can afford multiple readings. It can be understood as a critique of the socio-cultural situation of Tibet, or read as a depiction of an individual facing the moral degradation of society during its transition from tradition to modernity. Some readers might find in it a poignant reflection of the construction and dissolution of personal identity, perhaps even evoking a Sartrean existentialist echo.

The film

The film adaptation follows the basic structure of the short story, but there are significant additions and alterations. For one thing, the narrative scale of the film allows the story to be embellished with more details. A long scene is added in the photo studio in which Tharlo watches a couple take their wedding photos. After Tharlo returns to the mountain a sequence showing his solitary life is also added. On both his visits to the township scenes are added of Tharlo and Yangtso, the hairdresser, in the karaoke bar and nightclub. In terms of symbolic elements, two very important items are added, one being an orphaned lamb that functions almost as a symbolic double of Tharlo, the other being the firecrackers that Tharlo uses to protect his sheep but also to harm himself at the end. Only two scenes are removed from the short story. One is the banter between the police chief and the village chief at the beginning, and the other is that of Tharlo meeting some strangers in the street outside the photo studio.

More significant are the enrichments in the meaning of the story achieved by its imaginative treatment in the filmic medium. First, the connotation of the passage 'Serve the People' is more complex in the film, and its relevance is much more layered and nuanced. The film opens with a three-minute sequence of Tharlo intoning 'Serve the People' in Chinese in the style of a traditional Tibetan Buddhist chant. This comes as a surprise to the viewer, since Buddhist chant is the last form of recitation one would associate with this iconic Chinese Communist propaganda passage. The incongruity between the form of recitation and the content recited symbolises the differences between the two cultural value systems. In *Tharlo* tradition and modernity are not explored in their general terms, but in their specific manifestation in contemporary Tibet within the context of Communist China. Furthermore, an extra layer of this scene is added by the opening close-up of the lamb being fed from a bottle as Tharlo is reciting the passage. Tharlo brings his lamb with him everywhere, because being an orphan like himself, the lamb has lost its mother to a wolf. This image of the lamb as a symbol of the needy alerts the audience to the fact that the film not only tells a personal story but also a social one. The recitation of 'Serve the People' in full (although in a tone incongruous with the content) functions as a reminder of the Chinese Communist Party's claim to serve the people, to liberate the oppressed, and to help those in need, just as Tharlo cares for the lamb. However, this claim has fallen short of reality, and the discrepancy is suggested by other additions and alterations to the short story. Tharlo is required to remove his amulet when he has his photograph taken for the identity card; he is suspected of criminal wrongdoing when he fails to present his identity card to a policeman in town. Both incidents suggest that institutionalising everyday life is an intrusive action, the brunt of which is borne by the underprivileged. Moreover, when a newlywed couple have their photograph taken against a backdrop of Tian'anmen (at the photo studio where Tharlo is waiting to have his photograph taken), the tense expression on their faces—separated as they are by the portrait of Mao—suggests the pervasiveness of public politics. This oppressive atmosphere is further reinforced by the image of a barbed wire fence that spreads across the screen towards the end of the film, which echoes the final scene of *Old Dog*.[18]

Second, the loss of traditional values is still a focus of concern, but the past is a much more complex and ambiguous experience than depicted in the short story, or in any of Pema Tseden's previous films. Surely, the modern as embodied by Yangtso is represented as dangerous and

---

[18] The respective scenes in *Old Dog* and in *Tharlo* with the barbed wire fence were shot in the same location. It has not been possible for the editors to confirm whether it was a coincidence, or by intention, or out of practical convenience.

deceitful. She wears her hair short and smokes, both of which are considered unconventional by Tharlo. She has forgotten all the traditional Amdo Tibetan *la glu* (love songs) she learnt while herding sheep as a child, figuring as the latest in a line of young Tibetans—stretching back to Juga in *The Grassland*—who have turned away from traditional cultural values that are being eroded by the spread of capital under Communist patronage. Yangtso's act of deception is to a considerable degree a consequence of a predatory environment created by economic self-interest. However, traditional life in *Tharlo* is hardly the utopian past to which the protagonist wishes to cling or hopes to rediscover. Tharlo's life as a shepherd is far from being one of fulfilment and security. When his herd is attacked and some of his sheep lost to the wolves, he is abused by his employer and left to bear the loss himself. This combination of exploitation and humiliation has definitely triggered Tharlo's decision to run away with Yangtso. Unlike Pema Tseden's short story 'Where the Moon Rises', in which the past is where the beautiful white moon shines bright and covers everything in a silvery hue, in *Tharlo* the past and the future are not placed in binary opposition. Leaving the wolf attack aside, Tharlo's solitary existence is represented as being both tough and lonely.[19] In successive scenes after his return to the mountains following his first trip to town, he is framed in the narrow internal space of his mud hut, which only allows basic human activities to maintain survival. In exterior day scenes he is repeatedly placed in either parallel or contrasting positions with a scarecrow, the only other entity in the mountain that is shaped like a human but is devoid of humanity. In the night scenes he is shown in extremely wide shots outdoors as a tiny figure almost completely swallowed up by the darkness of the night. The only thing that comes close to human contact is the voice of another human being from his radio. Even without the dramatic event of the wolf attack, the camera has told the audience very clearly the basic facts of Tharlo's situation: the brave new world might be plagued with perils and even evils, but the past is no refuge for romantic nostalgia. The individual is not faced with a dichotomy of good (tradition) versus bad (modernity),

---

[19] In the shooting script there is a scene in the mountain in which Tharlo meets a girl whose lower face is covered by a scarf and who teaches him to sing *la glu*. This scene was shot but edited out in the final cut. In a discussion about the film with the editors Pema Tseden explained that this scene was cut in order to stress Tharlo's solitary existence on the mountain.

but with two equally unsatisfactory situations over which he is not empowered to have any control. This is a much more poignant, and also more realistic and critical, exploration of tradition and modernity than in any other of Pema Tseden's works so far. It is also a much more acute portrayal of the brutality inflicted on disempowered individuals than in any of Pema Tseden's previous works.

Indeed, in *Tharlo* the 'voice', as it were, of the camera angle is much more pronounced than in any of his previous films, and the result is the accentuation of a scopic effect that has created a symbolism of *looking* that is fundamental to the theme. *Tharlo* has been lauded for its bold cinematographic design. Three major cinematographic decisions have defined the structure of the film: long takes, static camera positions, and showing the *mise-en-scène* in mirror reflections. The three are executed together in every shot, not alternatively or separately in different shots. The entire film consists of fifty-one scenes but only eighty-seven shots, of which thirty-six are single-shot scenes. There is not a single camera movement in any of the shots. At least one-third of the scenes are shot entirely as mirror reflections. These require extremely skillful management of the *mise-en-scène* on the part of the director, akin to the stage organisation required of a stage director. Such design is not simply a showcase of skills. By adopting long takes and static camera positions, the film has eschewed *omniscient seeing* in multiple perspectives facilitated by montage and camera movements that have defined the narrative cinema. In place of this, a *limited seeing* is constructed in *Tharlo*, as the beholder—the camera—only sees an aspect, from one perspective. The shots are not point-of-view shots. Instead, they are positioned to accentuate the voyeuristic perspective of an onlooker, an outsider who sees, but from only one exterior perspective, the life of Tharlo and of Tibet.

In this connection it is interesting to compare Pema Tseden's photo-taking scene in *Tharlo* with *The Butter Lamp* by Hu Wei, a Han Chinese director based in Shanghai and Paris. *The Butter Lamp* is a fifteen-minute short released in 2013. There is little narrative except a stream of Tibetans in traditional clothes being arranged by a photographer to take photos in front of backdrops showing Beijing, Hong Kong, and other Westenised settings. Write-ups of this film in festival brochures describe it as a celebration of Tibetans maintaining their traditional ways of life in the face of the changing world. This might be what the film aspires to, but its effect is rather different. The Tibetans in the film are shown in a uniformly passive demeanor handled by the photographer in the film as the objects of photography against the visual symbols of modernity and globalisation depicted in the backdrops. The film's emphasis on the appearance of these people, which resembles early ethnographic photos, is unfortunate; even more unfortunate is the lack of attempt to explore their agency in dealing with the context of modernity and globalisation. All these render the visual images of the passive Tibetans in front of the camera superficial and essentialising. A very similar scene is arranged in *Tharlo* of a couple taking wedding photos in the photo studio as Tharlo enters. The couple begins the photo-shoot wearing traditional Tibetan clothes sitting in front of backdrops showing different sites from the Potala Palace to Tian'anmen Square. The last of these backdrops is a street scene of New York, and they are made to change their clothes to Western-style clothing. Like the people being photographed in *The Butter Lamp*, this couple appear at odds even in Western clothes with the images on the backdrop, but unlike the passive personas in *The Butter Lamp*, this couple participates in shaping their situation by expressing their responses to the photographer's instructions. They notice Tharlo's lamb and ask to hold it in the last photo, and it is in this last photo that they look most natural. In this four-minute scene, the complex interplay between inhibition and agency of the objects of photography is thoroughly explored. If this scene is not intended as a spoof of *The Butter Lamp*,[20] at least it shows an in-depth contrast with the latter in its handling of a similar scenario and in understanding their common subject matters, namely, rural Tibetans' responses to urbanisation and globalisation. The contrast between the two scenes, although both rely completely on the scopic symbolism, is stark.

This motif of the scopic in *Tharlo* is further intensified by showing the *mise-en-scène* as mirror reflection. The majority of scenes in the township are shot as such, most predominantly in the mirrors of the barbershop

---

[20] When an extract of *The Butter Lamp* was shown in a discussion on *Tharlo* on 27th September, 2016 at the Weatherhead Centre, Columbia University with Pema Tseden present, he was surprised at the similarity in the two scenes, and indicated that he was not aware of the short film. Perhaps such similarity is neither surprising nor coincidental, since this kind of photo-taking activity is common among the rural Tibetan communities.

when Tharlo sits in the barber's chair, and when he and Yangtso talk outside the shop. The same arrangement is made for the scene in the township police station and the grocery store where he buys firecrackers and rice wine. In other street scenes his movements are shot as reflections in rear and side-view mirrors of vehicles. The exceptions are in the photo studio, the karaoke bar, and the night club. In the photo studio the position of the camera identifies with the camera within the story, which makes the scopic perspective more explicit. In the karaoke bar and the night club, the fairy lighting, the echoing effect of the microphone and the atmosphere already suggest a mood of performance and equivocation. These effects work well in place of the *illusory seeing* created by the mirror image, and creates a powerful symbolism of the scopic: Tharlo only sees the appearance of things and people in the township. There is no way for him to tell reality from illusion. Truth is often the exact opposite of what it seems. This can certainly be read as a critique of the modernised township, in which things and people, being subject to the influence and impetus of *development*, are not what they seem. This critique is also reflected in the representation of Tharlo's subjective state. In his own world of certainty at the beginning of the story, everything is seen as reality in the police station. He walks under the pipes of the iron stove creating the optical illusion of framing, but the image is undistorted. However, in the penultimate scene back in the police station, when his unambiguous world view and belief have been subverted, he can no longer recite Mao's text, and the Chinese slogan 'Serve the People' reflected in the mirror is now reversed.

Reading the use of mirror reflection as an acute critique of the reality of modernisation correlates with the critique that Pema Tseden has already engaged with in his previous films. Yet, such a reading would leave one mirror scene unexplained: up in the mountain after the wolf attack, Tharlo's employer abuses and slaps him. He leaves a dead lamb for Tharlo to eat and drives away. His face in the driver's seat is seen in the side mirror of the truck. With this one shot the dichotomy, as formalised by the use of the mirror reflection, expresses a contrast not only between the mountain and the township, but also one between Tharlo-on-his-own and Tharlo-with-other-people. The police chief, Yangtso, the grocer and Tharlo's employer impose on him the forces of institution, desire, consumption and exploitation respectively. These threats inflicted on the Self by the Others carry a Sartrean overtone depicting the Other as Hell (as in the latter's *Huis Clos*), and adds another dimension to Tharlo's story: the condition faced by Tharlo is social on one level, and ontological in nature and universal in relevance on another.

In *Tharlo* the portrayal of its protagonist's Self has a strong existentialist emphasis, and the mountain scenes, situating him among the vast expanse of mountains together with the flock of sheep, constitute powerful phenomenological images of that existentialist solitude. If the film were to stop short at this symbolism, it would be no more than a reiteration of Sartre's depiction of the human condition, and would offer nothing new to the universal theme embodied in his philosophical thesis. However, in *Tharlo* Pema Tseden offers us a visionary insight—though a soberly realist one—about the human condition. He sees the plight of the individual in his social and existential situation, but he also sees the possibility of compassion. If Tharlo is simply seen as the victim of the world, the Self and the Other will always be locked in an antagonistic dualism; but if we can shift our perspective and empathise with Tharlo's Other, a very different picture will emerge. This change of perspective and need to empathise with the Other is fully explored in the characterisation of Yangtso. She is the cause and agent of Tharlo's trouble, but she is also a victim of her circumstances. Like Tharlo, she is desperate to get out of the township. In the scene of the karaoke bar a most moving moment is created when she pours her heart out in the song *I Want to Leave the Mountains*. She sings off key, in an untrained voice, but imbues the song with a passionate life-force. This is the voice of a desperate young woman from a provincial township to whom life has not offered much. Subsequently, in the scene in the nightclub a coarse man intrudes on her and Tharlo in a familiar way, and both the man and Tharlo behave as if each has a claim on her. If Tharlo is the victim of the capitalist social order of *development*, Yangtso is doubly victimised by the capitalist and the patriarchal orders. Her aspiration to find a better life can only be fulfilled by an act of deceit. This reverse perspective is essential in *Tharlo*. Failing to see this structure might result in mistaking the film as misogynist. Yangtso is both culprit and victim in the story, as too is Tharlo. After the wolf attack, having been abused by his employer, Tharlo cuts up the dead sheep his employer has left for him. This scene is composed of a series of overhead shots revealing fully the bowels of the sheep with Tharlo hovering over the carcass dissecting and gutting it. In the next scene he sits by the stove eating the mutton. Tharlo in these two scenes is no longer the victim, but the victimiser of the sheep, a creature that is even lower down the food-chain than he is. What follows, but is not shown, is Tharlo selling the sheep that do not belong to him, and by this act he victimises the owner of the sheep. These two acts of killing and theft turn Tharlo into a 'bad person', and no different to Yangtso on a moral scale. Thus, if the audience of the film can sympathise with Tharlo, they are also required to sympathise with Yangtso.

This shift in point-of-view evokes the sense of fluidity of people's positions in *The Silent Holy Stones* and *The Search* in which the characters swap positions. In *Tharlo*, as in the earlier two films, Pema Tseden repeatedly makes his point against any fixity of positioning and identity. At the beginning of the story, Tharlo knows very well who he is. Ironically it is during the process of institutionalising his identity by issuing him an identity card—so that 'other people will know who he is' —that he becomes changed and lost. He goes all the way to the township to get his photo taken, but when the photo is put on the identity card, he no longer resembles the man in the photo. All these attempts to establish identity by providing proof fail. Like the actress in *The Search*[21], Tharlo is also seeking love. But unlike the actress whose lover has made himself unavailable to her, Tharlo's lover is available to him; the problem is that he does not see her clearly. He is flattered by her attention and praise, and excited to be interpellated into 'Tharlo' by her, as she expresses preference for his name over his nickname, although his nickname 'Ponytail' being a direct description of his hair is less arbitrary as a sign-name. In the end what he sees is not what she is. Appearance is not reality, in the same way that the photo is not the person, and therefore the identity card has nothing to do with who Tharlo is. On the one hand,

---

[21] The intertextual connection between Tharlo and the actress in *The Search* is firmly established in the shooting script of *Tharlo*. In one of the scenes of Tharlo's life on the mountain, he meets a shepherdess who teaches him to sing the *la glu*. The shepherdess wears a scarf to cover her lower face, and appears almost a muse of love, creating an allusion to the actress in *The Search*. This scene was cut out during editing in order to emphasise Tharlo's solitary existence in the mountain. Instead, the protagonist learns the *la glu* from the radio. The symbolism of love as undefinable reality embodied by the girl whose face cannot be seen would have been a striking allusion to *The Search* had this scene been kept in the film.

this offers the critique that so-called reality is elusive, even illusory; but on the other, it is exactly this elusiveness and instability of identity and positioning that allows perspectives to be shifted. If positions can be reversed and identities annulled, one would be more capable of looking at one's Other with empathy and compassion. Indeed it is compassion which endows the doubles of Tharlo and Yangtso—the newlyweds at the photography studio—with the possibility of hope. The couple, in traditional Tibetan dress, look stiff against the backdrop of New York City; their unnaturalness is not mitigated by donning Western-style clothes. The husband and wife, who used to be shepherds, are only able to relax with the lamb sitting in the wife's lap as she feeds it from a bottle, even though being photographed with an orphan is considered an inauspicious start to a marriage. The natural smile on their faces connotes compassion for the needy, the essence of what Buddhism—stripped of its accretions of superstition—stands for.

In Pema Tseden's films hope is not a matter of plausibility, but a belief system. It is not justified by plot or logic, but remains obstinately present. It is true that the ending of *Tharlo* is even grimmer than that of *Old Dog*. Whereas Akku in *Old Dog* kills the mastiff in an act of self-dispossession, Tharlo explodes a firecracker in his hand in an act of self-destruction. Whereas a long tracking shot of Akku reveals a landscape of green grassland, majestic mountains, white clouds and a blue sky, Tharlo is seen against a similar background, but in black and white and from a fixed camera position, as if the sense of his bleak predicament can only be captured negatively, through the absence of colour and movement. This cinematographic style, which is consistently used throughout *Tharlo*, is an attempt to take a long hard look at reality. The final shot of the firecracker exploding in Tharlo's grip abruptly cuts to black, evoking a violent and destructive feeling, but even in the bleakest of hours, a sense of hope, however faint, is instilled in the text. Even though Tharlo and Yangtso have not suceeded in building a life together with dignity and decency, their double—the couple in the photo studio—might do. The future of Tibet, and of the individuals, is still open, despite the travails brought to them in times of upheaval. Read as palimpsest, *Tharlo*, like his previous films, stages revisitations that resist narrative closure and construct an identity that is both open and dynamic. A sense of self is explored through the constant change of perspective, critical reflection and the expansion of experience, as characters engage with issues such as tradition and modernity, the spiritual and the mundane, love and compassion. It is this process of exploration and discovery that enables Pema Tseden's *Tharlo*, as well as his earlier films, to inspire his Tibetan and other audiences with a sense of agency and a capacity for transformation.

The film's equal relevance to Pema Tseden's Tibetan and non-Tibetan audience alike owes much to his mastery of the cinematic medium which shows greater sophistication than witnessed in any of his previous films. Theoretically, the short story, as an expression of the symbolic order of language, has an edge over the visual medium of the cinema in translating images of life into ideas, abstractions and typologies, hence the construction of allegories of universal pertinence. In contrast, the film, belonging to the iconic order of meaning and expressed through a visual medium, carries an inherent tendency for naturalism, hence realistic references are always highlighted. In terms of its generic attributes, the short story does not afford a narrative scale comparable with the novel. Its disadvantage in plot-scope and descriptive detail is paradoxically also its advantage in focusing on the momentary and the axiomatic, again facilitating an allegorical approach to its creation and interpretation. The outstanding example of this phenomenon can, of course, be found in the tales of Franz Kafka. Films also differ from novels in not having the capacity for a novelistic plot; at the same time, their propensity for naturalistic detail in each and every frame is telling, and contributes to the medium's natural proclivity for a specific and contextualised denotation of the *mise-en-scène*. In Pema Tseden's previous films this realistic-contextual proclivity of cinema has fostered a definite Tibetan specificity that is necessary to their themes. In *Tharlo* we see for the first time how this specificity has been turned to subtler effect. Compared to the dominance of full and medium shots in *Old Dog*, framing the characters in the mountains and the run-down township, or to the distinctive Tibetan Buddhist signifying networks of *The Silent Holy Stones* and *The Search*, *Tharlo* is minimalist in both its environmental and its cultural detail. The Tibetan concerns are always present, since these provide the setting and circumstances of the story from which all issues implicit in the film originate. However, the more psychological ambience and symbolic use of filmic language, as discussed earlier, promote its allegorical and universal relevance. Tharlo's existential solitude is pertinent to the film's audience within and beyond Tibet; and *hope*, connected with the Buddhist idea of *compassion*, is Pema Tseden's contribution, from his position of Tibetan Buddhism, to the exploration in international cinema of this universal theme. *Tharlo* is Pema Tseden's first film in which interpretive extension from the specific to the general is fully facilitated, and it is precisely this interpretive extension that inspires human empathy and intellectual reflection. Such a film reminds us that what we perceive as the plight of others is in fact a specific case of the general human state, and that no one is beyond and above such predicament. This reminder is particularly valuable to all of us living in the modern world, in which complacent apathy toward other people's suffering increasingly dominates the popular media and public policies. It is for this reason that *Tharlo* and Pema Tseden's other works deserve attention both from fellow-Tibetans and from an international audience.

References

Benjamin, Walter. 1992. *Illuminations*. Translated by Harry Zohn. London: Fontana Press.

Bergson, Henri. 1911. *Laughter: An Essay on the Meaning of the Comic*. Translated by Cloudesley Brereton and Fred Rothwell. London: Macmillan.

Erickson, Steven. 2013. 'High Plains Drifter'. *Sight and Sound* 23(6): 70.

Frangville, Vanessa. 2009. 'Tibet in Debate: Narrative Construction and Misrepresentations in *Seven Years in Tibet* and *Red River Valley*'. *Transtext(e)s-Transcultures – Journal of Global Cultural Studies*, May. http://transtexts.revues.org/289.

Genette, Gérard. 1997. *Palimpsests: Literature in the Second Degree*. Translated by Channa Newman and Claude Doubinsky. Lincoln: University of Nebraska Press.

Hansen, Peter. 2001. 'Tibetan Horizon: Tibet and the Cinema in the Early Twentieth Century'. In *Imagining Tibet: Perceptions, Projections, and Fantasies*. Edited by Thierry Dodin and Heinz Räther. Boston: Wisdom Publications. 91–110.

Harvey, Dennis. 2006. 'The Silent Holy Stones'. *Variety* 402(13): 34.

Higgins, Dick. 2001. 'Intermedia'. *Leonardo* 34(1): 49–54.

Horton, Andrew and Stuart McDougal. 1998. *Play It Again, Sam: Retakes on Remakes*. Berkeley: University of California Press.

Kerr, Elizabeth. 2014. 'The Sacred Arrow: Shanghai Review'. *The Hollywood Reporter*, 19th June. http://www.hollywoodreporter.com/review/sacred-arrow-shanghai-review-713053.

Lee, Maggie. 2014. 'Film Review: *The Sacred Arrow*'. *Variety*, 2nd July. http://variety.com/2014/film/asia/film-review-the-sacred-arrow-1201257308/.

Lo, Kwai-Cheung. 2013. 'Reconfiguring the Chinese Diaspora through the Eyes of Ethnic Minorities'. In *Diasporic Chineseness after the Rise of China: Communities and Cultural Production*. Edited by Julia Kuehn, Kam Louie, and David Pomfret. Vancouver: University of British Columbia Press. 170–186.

Pema Tseden. 2006. *The Master in Tibet* [*Dashi zai xizang*]. Lanzhou: Lanzhou University Press.

----. 2011. *The Dream of the Wandering Singer* [*Liulang geshou de meng*]. Lhasa: Tibet People's Press.

----. 2014. *Holy Stones, Quietly Chiseled* [*Manishi, jingjingde qiao*]. Beijing: China Nationalities Arts Press.

----. 2014. *The Colour of Death* [*Siwang de yanse*]. Beijing: Zuojia Press.

----. 2016. *Tharlo* [*Taluo*]. Guangzhou: Huacheng Press.

----. 2017.'Where the Moon Rises'. Translated by Jessica Yeung. *Voice and Verse Poetry* 34-35: 142-143.

----. 2017.'Her Ninth Man'. Translated by Jessica Yeung. *Cha: An Asian Literary Journal*, March. http://www.asiancha.com/content/view/2687/605/.

Stam, Robert. 2005. *Literature Through Film: Realism, Magic, and the Art of Adaptation*. Malden, MA: Blackwell.

Williams, Raymond. 1993. *Drama from Ibsen to Brecht*. London: The Hogarth Press.

དེ་འོས་པ་ཞིག་རེད། མི་དཔལ་ལ་ནས་འདེབས་བུ་མེར་རེད།

That's our job. We serve the people.

གཡ་ཤིན་རང་སྤོ་པ་བུ་ཀྱོ་ར་བ་ཞེས་ཡིན་ཞོ། གཅིག་ཀྱང་འཇེད་མི་སྲིད། །

I remember everything I've learnt. I don't forget a thing.

ཁར་རང་ཉིད་ཀྱིས་ཤུ་ཤེག་ཡིན་པ་དེས་ཉེན་པར་མི་ཚོག་གམ།

Isn't it enough that I know who I am?

.

>> The Short Story

Tharlo

Tharlo had always had a ponytail. It bounced around on the back of his head in such a way that you couldn't miss it. He'd had it for as long as anyone could remember, so people just called him 'Ponytail'. Nobody could remember his real name.

Earlier in the year the township police had called a meeting with the entire village. Everyone was required to register for a new identity card. When Tharlo's turn came, the police chief repeated his name several times, but he wasn't there to answer. The police chief turned to the village chief, 'Is there anyone named Tharlo here?'

The village chief gave it some thought and said, 'It's unlikely we have anyone by that name here.'

The police chief said with a stern face, 'I'm not asking whether it's likely. You have to tell me definitively whether such a person lives here.'

The village chief racked his brain but couldn't recall anyone by that name. He finally said, 'Our village has hundreds of inhabitants. I can't remember everyone.'

The police chief looked directly at him and asked, 'Then how can you manage as their village chief?'

The village chief became agitated. 'The job of a village chief isn't to remember everyone's name. My job is to bring the entire village *out of poverty onto the road of prosperity*. On top of that, there is the exploding birth rate. These women in our village keep pumping out babies. They don't care about the fine. We're talking about five or six births in just the last couple of days. How can I remember all of their names? Some of them don't even have names yet.'

The police chief smiled. 'You are the village chief. You should remember everyone's name.'

The village chief gave the police chief a stern look. 'Do you remember the names of everyone registered in your police station?'

'That is a different matter. You are the chief of your village.'

'And you are the chief of your police station.'

The police chief smiled. 'If you don't know this person, then I'll delete him from the list. But, if ever he finds himself denied accommodation in town, don't blame me.'

At this point the village chief smiled. He signaled the village bookkeeper to come over and asked him, 'Is there a Tharlo in our village?'

The bookkeeper was a middle-aged man. He gave it some thought, but couldn't recall anyone by that name.

He looked at the village chief and the police chief, both waiting for him to answer. He decided that further help was needed, and called upon the chief of their production team.

The bookkeeper asked the chief of the production team, 'Do you know anyone named Tharlo in our village?'

The chief of the production team gave it some serious thought, and then started laughing. 'Yes, of course, you mean Ponytail!'

Both the village chief and the bookkeeper joined in his delight. They both said, 'Yes, of course, Ponytail. That's right. Tharlo is Ponytail, and Ponytail is Tharlo. The same person. We'd nearly forgotten about him.'

The police chief looked at them, slightly puzzled.

The village chief explained to him, 'Ponytail is Tharlo's nickname. We all call him by his nickname, and had simply forgotten his real name!'

The police chief asked, 'Where is he now?'

The village chief said, 'This is the thing. He grew up an orphan. No one could care for him. So, years ago he took on the job of herding sheep in the mountains for families in the village. They pay him for that. Since then he's been living by himself in the mountains. I have no idea who started calling him that, but it's what everyone has called him since he was a teenager.'

'He has to come in person to take a photo for his identity card. You have to go and get him.'

'Must the photo be taken today?'

'Not today. But he'll have to come to the township to have it done.'

'In that case I'll look into getting him to come into town. It'll take a couple of days.'

It was approximately ten days later that Tharlo went to the township police station.

When the police chief saw his ponytail tied up with a red piece of thread, he asked him, 'You must be Ponytail?'

Tharlo was surprised. He looked at the police chief and asked, 'How did you know?'

The police chief smiled. 'We policemen naturally know more than other people.'

With a touch of admiration, Tharlo said, 'No wonder, you've been able to catch some of the bad people.'

The police chief laughed. 'Do you mean that there are some bad people we haven't caught?'

'That's right. The year before last I had three ewes and nine lambs stolen. You didn't manage to catch that thief.'

'Did you report the theft?'

'Of course I did. I asked the village chief to do it for me.'

'He's a busy man. Perhaps he forgot.'

'Maybe. But later on I asked him, and he swore to me he had been here to report it.'

'There are many incidents like that. Losing a few sheep here and there.'

'On the other hand, last year a thief stole twelve of my sheep, and you caught him just one month later. You really are good.'

The police chief couldn't help laughing and said, 'When you lose that many at one time, obviously we have to do something.'

Now Tharlo was filled with admiration. 'You found them one month after they were stolen. That was impressive.'

Still laughing, but responding to Tharlo's admiration, the police chief replied with an air of humility, 'That is our job. We serve the people.'

Tharlo laughed, too. 'I know that saying. Chairman Mao said that. I learnt it in primary school.'

The police chief looked at Tharlo, as though now seeing him in a fresh light. 'You went to school?'

Tharlo looked quite serious. 'Of course I went to school. I went to primary school and my grades were good. I learnt *Serve the People* by heart.'

'Did you? Do you still remember it?'

'Of course I do. I remember everything I've learnt. I don't forget a thing.'

'Well, then, why not recite it for me?'

Tharlo paused for a moment and then began reciting, '*Serve The People.* Eighth of September, nineteen forty-four. Mao Zedong. Our Communist Party and the Eighth Route and New Fourth Armies led by our Party are battalions of our revolution. These battalions of ours are wholly dedicated to the liberation of the people and work entirely in the people's interests. Comrade Zhang Side was in the ranks of these battalions.

'All men must die, but death can vary in its significance. The ancient Chinese writer Sima Qian said: *Though death befalls all men alike, it may be weightier than Mount Tai or lighter than a feather.* To die for the people is weightier than Mount Tai, but to work for the fascists and die for the exploiters and oppressors is lighter than a feather. Comrade Zhang Side died for the people, and his death is indeed weightier than Mount Tai.

'If we have shortcomings, we are not afraid to have them pointed out and criticised, because we serve the people. Anyone, no matter who, may point out our shortcomings. If he is right, we will correct them. If what he proposes will benefit the people, we will act upon it. The idea of *better troops and simpler administration* was put forward by Mr Li Dingming, who is not a Communist. He made a good suggestion which is of benefit to the people, and we have adopted it. If, in the interests of the people, we persist in doing what is right and correct what is wrong, our ranks will surely thrive.

'We hail from all corners of the country and have joined together for a common revolutionary objective. And we need the vast majority of a people with us on the road to this objective. Today, we already lead base areas with a population of ninety-one million, but this is not enough; to liberate the whole nation more are needed. In times of difficulty we must not lose sight of our achievements, must see the bright future and must pluck up our courage. The Chinese people are suffering; it is our duty to serve them and we must exert ourselves in struggle. Wherever there is struggle there is sacrifice, and death is a common occurrence. But we have the interests of the people and the sufferings of the great majority at heart, and when we die for the people it is a worthy death. Nevertheless, we should do our best to avoid unnecessary sacrifices. Our cadres must show concern for every soldier, and all people in the revolutionary ranks must care for each other, must love and help each other.

'From now on, when anyone in our ranks who has done some useful work dies, be he soldier or cook, we should have a funeral ceremony and a memorial meeting in his honour. This should become the rule. And it should be introduced among the people as well. When someone dies in a village, let a memorial meeting be held. In this way we express our mourning for the dead and unite all the people.'[1]

Tharlo recited the entire piece without having to stop and think. When he finished, the police chief was staring at him open-mouthed.

Tharlo asked, 'How was it? Did I make any mistakes?'

Only then was the police chief able to recover and resume his normal expression. 'I didn't know you were a genius!'

Tharlo didn't think he was, so he said, 'I just have a slightly better memory than other people.'

'When did you learn this?'

'When I was fourteen. I was in primary school. Back then all the texts in our books were taken from the works of Chairman Mao. I can recite many other works by him.'

'You really are a clever fellow. How old are you?'

'Twenty-nine.'

The police chief murmured a few more words of praise for Tharlo before saying, 'If I had a memory like yours, I would have gone to university.'

'I stopped after primary school. My parents died young. My relatives didn't want to take care of me. They said that I had a good memory, and that I should look after sheep for a few households and herd them in the mountains. They also told me I only needed to remember the colour and

---

1   This translation of 'Serve the People' is the PRC's official translation. *Selected Works of Mao Tse-tung Volume III*. 1965. Beijing: Foreign Languages Press. Translator unspecified. The transliteration of 'Mao Zedong', 'Zhang Side' and 'Sima Qian' has been updated to the *pinyin* system by the present translator.

markings of each sheep. If I didn't lose any sheep, I could make a living at it. There were no other openings for me, so I took the sheep to the mountains. I started with one hundred and thirty-six. The second year I had sixteen more. The third year I had forty-seven more. The fourth year I had only eleven more. That year we had a bad snowstorm. It killed many lambs. In any case, every year I have more sheep. There hasn't been a single year that I've had fewer. Now I have as many as three hundred and seventy-five; of them two hundred and nine are white, seventy-one black, ninety-five mixed. One hundred thirty-four have horns, two hundred forty-one don't.'

Again, the police chief was amazed. After regaining his composure, he said, 'What a waste! What a waste! This is such a waste of someone like you!'

Tharlo said, 'The way I think about it is that I'm also serving the people by herding their sheep, although they pay me about a dozen sheep every year, and also some money.'

The policeman was quick to nod his head in agreement. 'Yes, of course, of course.'

'I like what Chairman Mao said about death: *Though death befalls all men alike, it may be weightier than Mount Tai or lighter than a feather.*'

The police chief resumed his normal expression. 'Look, you certainly have remembered the piece accurately, but you haven't really understood it, have you? Chairman Mao didn't say that, Sima Qian said that. Sima Qian was a great writer.'

'Is that so? How were Chairman Mao and Sima Qian related?'

The police chief laughed. 'They weren't related. Sima Qian lived in ancient times. Chairman Mao lived in modern times. There wasn't much of a relationship between them.'

Tharlo didn't quite understand, and asked him, 'Then what about this part: *To die for the people is weightier than Mount Tai, but to work for the fascists and die for the exploiters and oppressors is lighter than a feather. Comrade Zhang Side died for the people, and his death is indeed weightier than*

Mount Tai? Chairman Mao did say that, didn't he?'

'Yes, that he did say.'

'How come they talked so alike?'

'They both meant the same thing.'

'I herd sheep for people in our village. Will my death be weightier than Mount Tai, like Zhang Side's?'

'Yes, definitely. Your death will certainly be weightier than Mount Tai, like Zhang Side's, but don't worry, that's still a long way off. In any case I can tell you are a good person, a good person like Zhang Side.'

'How can you tell I'm a good person like Zhang Side?'

'We can tell good people from bad with a single glance. We policemen might not be experts in everything, but when it comes to that, we know what we're doing.'

'Can you explain to me how you tell good people from bad?'

The police chief gave him a mysterious smile. 'This I can't tell you. It's how we earn our keep.'

Tharlo was slightly disappointed. But, at the same time, he couldn't hide the admiration in his eyes.

The police chief repeated his praise, 'You certainly have a good memory!'

Tharlo suddenly remembered why he had come, and said, 'I'm here to have a photograph taken. Our village chief sent me.'

The police chief looked askance, and gave him a harsh look from the corner of his eye. 'Why did it take you so long? The photographer is gone.'

'Our village chief found someone to take over for me only yesterday. I came as soon as I could.'

'Now you'll have to go to the township to have your photo taken.'

'Must I?'

'Yes, you must. It is for your identity card.'

'What's an identity card?'

'When you go into town, people will know who you are by looking at your identity card. They will know where you come from.'

'Isn't it enough that I know who I am?'

At this moment the police chief seemed to be recalling something. 'What is your name?'

'Ponytail.'

'No, your real name.'

Tharlo thought about it for a moment. 'Tharlo.'

'Tharlo, yes. Go into the town today. Look for Dekyi Photo Studio. There is a woman there called Dekyi. Say that you have been sent by the police for a photo. She'll know what to do.'

Tharlo smiled. 'This real name of mine doesn't feel like mine at all. It sounds strange to my own ears.'

The police chief looked at the watch on his wrist. 'Don't waste your time talking. Go on. You can still catch the bus to town.'

Tharlo caught the bus and arrived in town.

When he got off the bus and found himself walking along the street in town, he felt slightly unsettled and nervous. He looked at everybody rushing around and had no idea which way to go.

He saw a primary school child with a red scarf walking past. He stopped him and asked, 'Little friend, do you know where Dekyi Photo Studio is?'

The primary school child stared at him, then at his ponytail, and shook his head vigorously.

Tharlo said to him, 'Little friend, don't be frightened. My name is Ponytail. I need to go to Dekyi Photo Studio to have a photo taken.'

The school child was now amused. 'If you let me look at your ponytail, I'll take you there.'

Tharlo squatted down quite happily, so that the boy could have a look at his ponytail.

The school child showed great interest in Tharlo's ponytail. 'Our teacher said only people in the Manchurian dynasty wore ponytails. Why do you still have one?'

Tharlo looked at the school child and said to him, 'Do you really think I'm from the Manchurian dynasty!'

The school child said, 'I'll have to ask my teacher.'

Tharlo got up. 'Now, will you take me to Dekyi Photo Studio?'

The school child suddenly grew nervous again. 'I don't remember exactly where it is.'

Tharlo grew desperate. He took out a ten-*yuan*[2] note.

'Take me there and I'll give you this.'

---

[2]   1 Chinese *yuan* is approximately equivalent to 0.11 pounds sterling or 15 cents in U.S. dollars.

The school child promptly took him straight to the door of Dekyi Photo Studio. Clutching the ten-*yuan* note, the child dashed into the adjacent snack shop.

Tharlo opened the door and entered. He saw a woman taking a photo of a man. Next to them sat several other people. As soon as the man had forced his features into an unnatural smile, a clicking noise was heard from the camera. Then the man got up and went to one side. One of the men sitting on the side went over, sat on the same stool and straightened his back.

Tharlo went inside. The woman didn't greet him and continued working.

Tharlo stayed by the door and asked, 'Is this Dekyi Photo Studio?'

The woman turned to him. 'Yes, this is Dekyi Photo Studio. Can I help you?'

'I'm here to see Dekyi.'

The woman stopped what she was doing and looked at Tharlo with suspicion. She said to him, 'I'm Dekyi.'

Tharlo gave her a faint smile. 'I've come to have a photo taken. The police chief sent me.'

'Do you want a passport photo?'

'I don't know. He said it was for some sort of card.'

Dekyi smiled. 'Why didn't you say so? That's a passport photo. It's for the identity card. The way you go on! I was wondering what you wanted. Take a seat. These people are all here for passport photos.'

They all smiled at Tharlo. He sat down next to them.

When they were all finished and had gone, Dekyi signaled Tharlo to come over. 'Now it's your turn.'

Tharlo went over and sat on the same stool in front of the white background.

Dekyi approached him with a camera in her hand. She looked at Tharlo's ponytail as if at some new discovery. 'Why do you have a ponytail?'

'I've had it since I was very young.'

'You can't take your photo like this, can you?'

'Why not?'

'Well, you see, the police station won't be able to tell whether you are a man or a woman.'

Tharlo became very serious. 'I was just at the police station. The police chief didn't say anything about that.'

'Well, that's fine then. I'll just take your photo.'

Tharlo straightened up his back just as the other men had done before him. He was just about to force a smile.

Dekyi tried a few positions with her camera. She also went over to Tharlo and tried to tidy up his hair. Then she said, 'I suggest you have your hair washed first. It's too messy now. You aren't going to look very good in the photo.'

'I don't mind if it's messy. I'm not fussy.'

It was Dekyi's turn to be serious. 'You'll use this identity card for the rest of your life. Don't you want to look good in the photo?'

Tharlo looked at Dekyi and said nothing.

She pointed to a barbershop across the road. 'Get your hair washed there. The owner is a good friend of mine.'

Tharlo unenthusiastically got up and walked out of the photo studio.

As Tharlo entered the barbershop, a girl with short hair stood up to greet him.

He looked at her with curiosity, and asked, 'Are you the good friend of Dekyi over there? I'm here to have my hair washed.'

The shorthaired girl gave him a long stare, and then let him sit in the barber's chair. She stood behind him, her eyes fixed on his face in the mirror. 'Do you want a wet or dry wash? Five *yuan* for a wet wash, ten for a dry wash.'

He looked back at her in the mirror. 'What do you mean by a dry wash?'

She smiled. 'That's washing without water.'

'How do you wash something without water?'

'It's nice. You'll understand if you try it.'

'Then I'll have a dry wash.'

She took a shampoo cream and squeezed some onto his head, and then started gently rubbing it into his hair.

Tharlo kept watching her in the mirror.

She looked back at his image in the mirror. 'The dry wash is nice, isn't it?'

'It is.'

'You haven't washed your hair for quite a while, have you?' She was trying to make conversation.

'I herd sheep. I don't have all that much water to wash my hair.'

She put on a deliberate look of surprise. 'Oh, really? Well then, how many sheep do you have?'

He said without giving it a second thought, 'I have three hundred and seventy-five in total, of them one hundred thirty-three are wethers, one hundred sixty-eight, ewes, seventy-four, half-grown lambs. Of the one hundred and sixty-eight ewes, one hundred and twenty-four will give lambs this year. Forty-four are too old to breed.'

She stopped rubbing his hair and looked at him in amazement, still in front of her in the mirror. 'You have a good memory!'

Tharlo never thought much about his own memory. 'I must remember everything about all of the sheep, so that I can take proper care of them.'

She started rubbing his hair again, still eying him in the mirror. 'How much are all those sheep worth?'

'I sold two on the way here today. They gave me six hundred *yuan*. Now it is about two hundred *yuan* for a ewe, probably a bit more if she is pregnant, around two fifty, maybe. Altogether my sheep should be worth about eighty to ninety thousand.'

Her mouth opened slightly in surprise. 'That much?'

'But not all three hundred seventy-five sheep belong to me. Only about one hundred are mine.'

'That's still quite a lot.'

She took Tharlo to sit under a tap to rinse his hair.

Tharlo asked as she was rinsing his hair, 'Didn't you say dry wash? Why are you using water?'

She smiled. 'The wash is dry, but the rinse requires water.'

Tharlo didn't say anything else.

When she was done, she let him sit back in the chair in front of the mirror, and started drying his hair with an electric hair dryer.

Tharlo stared at her in the mirror.

She smiled and continued to dry his hair. 'Why are you looking at me like that? Do I look that good?'

'I thought you were a man when I came in. Then I saw your earrings.'

She gave a brief laugh. 'Short hair is trendy in the city. This is in fashion.'

'But you're a Tibetan girl. Tibetan girls should keep their hair long.'

She laughed again, 'I cut my hair short because I'm waiting for boys with long hair to come find me.'

Tharlo didn't know what to say. He moved his eyes away from the girl's face and started looking around.

When she finished drying his hair, she put her hand on his shoulder and looked at him in the mirror again. There was a touch of warmth and easiness in her voice as she said to him, 'Look, with a bit of care you could be really cute.'

Tharlo was embarrassed. He quickly took out a fifty-*yuan* note from his satchel and handed it to her. 'Here.'

She took the note. 'Don't you have anything smaller? I don't have change.'

'Don't worry, just keep it.'

Before she could say anything, he dashed from the shop.

He crossed the road and went back to the photo studio. Just as he was about to enter, a few people went in ahead of him. He hung around by the door, and took out a cigarette to smoke.

He took a puff of the cigarette and looked across the road at the barbershop. He could see the shorthaired girl through the window. She looked back and gave him a smile.

Right then a group of young people walked past. They were most likely university students. One of them came toward him and tried to strike up a conversation.

'We're university students from the Mainland. We're here on holiday. You look unusual. Are you an artist?'

Tharlo was puzzled. He kept smoking and staring at the young student. He had no idea what he was talking about. His facial expression was quite serious.

Another spoke. 'Look at his eyes. They're so deep. He must be an artist of great depth.'

Tharlo paid no attention. He finished his cigarette and chucked the butt on the floor. Then he stamped on it to put it out. 'Actually, I herd sheep.'

Another one spoke. 'Listen to him! He's so deep. He's definitely an artist.'

At this point the people came out of the photo studio. Tharlo went in.

As soon as Dekyi saw him enter, she said, 'Well, well, well, you look very different with just a little bit of cleaning-up! Aren't you cute now?'

Tharlo was embarrassed by her praise. He walked directly over to sit on the stool in front of the white background.

She walked over to him with her camera, making adjustments to the settings on her way. 'Do you want a fast photo or a slow photo?'

Tharlo was confused. 'What is a fast photo and what is a slow photo?'

'A fast photo is ready today. A slow photo will be ready tomorrow.'

'I'll have a fast one.'

'Twenty *yuan* for a fast one, ten for slow.'

'That's fine. I'll have a fast one.'

She aimed the camera at him and clicked.

With that done, she walked over to the desk on the side and said to Tharlo, who was still sitting on the stool, 'You pay over here.'

He walked over and took out another fifty-*yuan* note. 'Do you have change?'

She glanced at the note, and, with a brief 'yes', began rummaging through the drawer. 'I just saw you talking to some lads outside. What did they want?'

'They asked whether I was an artist.'

Dekyi gave him a long look and said with a big smile, 'Did they?'

'Yes, they did. That was what they asked.'

Dekyi gave him another big smile, 'What did you say to them?'

'I told them I herd sheep.'

This time Dekyi laughed.

'What is an artist?'

She smiled again. 'Artists are people who grow their hair long and have a ponytail, just like yours.'

He looked at her, genuinely puzzled. She found the correct number of small notes for his change and handed them to him. 'Come back in half an hour to pick up your photo.'

Once again Tharlo went outside the studio to smoke. The shorthaired girl came out from her shop. 'You smoke.'

'Yes, I smoke.'

'I was watching you through the window. You really are cute.'

Tharlo felt nervous. He started smoking another cigarette as soon as he finished the first one.

'Let's go to a bar tonight and have some fun.'

'I've never been.'

'It's fun. I'm sure loads of girls will like you. You're cute.'

Tharlo felt nervous again.

The thirty minutes finally passed and Tharlo went to pick up his photo. He unwrapped it and looked at his own portrait. He blurted out, 'I look terrible!'

That night Tharlo drank a lot in a very noisy bar. When he woke in the morning, he found the shorthaired girl asleep by his side.

He felt uneasy and sat up. The girl woke up. She looked at him and smiled.

He didn't dare look her in the face. She spoke first. 'Do you like me?'

He was overcome with worry and sat there saying nothing.

'Last night you said you liked me.' She caressed his ponytail, 'I like your ponytail.'

He was nervous.

She put her head on his shoulder. 'Take me somewhere else. I don't want to stay here any longer.'

At last Tharlo found something to say, 'I've never been anywhere.'

'Then I'll take you to places. We can go to Lhasa, Beijing, Shanghai, Guangzhou and Hong Kong. Anywhere.'

'I've never thought about going to those places.'

'Where would you go if you were to choose?'

'Lhasa, of course.'

'Then we'll go to Lhasa.'

'People say that takes a lot of money. We don't have enough money.'

'Sell your sheep. Then we'll have money.'

'They aren't all mine. Some belong to other people.'

Tharlo arrived at the township police station around noon. The police chief saw him. 'One trip to town has made you much more handsome!'

Tharlo told him, 'I might have met a bad person.'

The police chief was alarmed. 'You have to report to us at once when you come across bad people.'

'Now, I can't be sure whether it really is a bad person.'

The police chief smiled. 'Ponytail, you must have proof when you report a bad person. Otherwise, you will bear the full legal responsibility.'

Tharlo felt like he was choking on something. He fell silent.

The police chief asked, 'Where is your photo?'

Tharlo took it out and gave it to him. 'I look terrible.'

'All passport photos look the same.'

Tharlo didn't say anything else.

The police chief put the photo away and registered it in his book. 'That's it. Come back in a month to pick up your card.'

Tharlo was about to get up from his seat and leave when the police chief spoke again, 'Let me ask you a personal question: why have you kept the ponytail?'

Tharlo straightened his back and began, 'This . . .'

The police chief was interested. 'This what . . . ?'

'There's no reason, really.'

The police chief was disappointed. 'It's fine if you don't want to tell me. It's your right not to.'

Tharlo looked at him. 'It's nothing important. It was just a film I saw.'

The police chief became interested again. 'What do you mean?'

'When I graduated from primary school, before I moved up to the mountains, I had some money from the people who had hired me to tend their sheep. I went into town.'

'And then?'

'I watched a movie there.'

'What does it have to do with your ponytail?'

'I grew it after watching the movie.'

'What is the connection?'

'There was a man with a ponytail in the movie. Women liked him.'

The police chief laughed out loud. 'Have you gotten women to like you since you've grown your ponytail?'

'Women in our village don't like me. They say I'm too poor.'

The police chief stopped laughing. 'What was the movie called?'

'I don't know. People said it was a foreign movie, so I went. Afterward, I told many people about the story. No one else said they'd seen it.'

The police chief said with regret, 'I must find time to see that movie.'

One month later, carrying a satchel on his shoulder, Tharlo went straight to the barbershop as soon as he arrived in town.

The shorthaired girl was cutting a male customer's hair. Tharlo sat down on a stool at the side. He looked at the girl in the mirror. She gave him a smile, also in the mirror, without turning to greet him.

When the man was gone, she said to him, still in the mirror, 'Your hair is dirty again. It's time for another wash.'

He walked over and sat in the chair that the other man had just been sitting in, and kept looking at her in the mirror.

Now she could see him clearly, and said, 'What's happened to you? You look so pale!'

He put his satchel on top of her box of hairdressing tools. 'There's ninety thousand *yuan* here.'

She placed both hands on his shoulder, and looked at his pale face in the mirror. 'Relax. Relax. Everything will be fine once you relax.'

He was silent and looked pale.

She said, 'Let me wash your hair.'

She squeezed out some shampoo and gently rubbed it into his hair.

He gradually relaxed and slowly closed his eyes. The colour on his face came back.

When he woke, she was sitting by his side looking at him.

'You were so worked up you fell asleep.'

He looked around with a dreamy expression on his face, and a dreamy look in his eyes.

'I've tied up your ponytail nice and neat.'

He continued to stare vacantly.

She passed a bottle of drinking water to him. 'Have some water.'

He unscrewed the lid and took a few sips.

She looked into his eyes. 'Now, there's one more thing you need to do for the two of us.'

He stared at her and took another sip of water.

She asked him, 'Would you?'

He took a big sip of water and made a gurgling noise in his throat as he swallowed. His throat felt unusually tight.

'Your ponytail gets too much attention. You've got to cut it.'

Tharlo stopped drinking the water and looked at himself in the mirror.

She looked back at him in the mirror. 'You agree, right?'

He continued to stare at his own face.

'If you like me with long hair, I'll grow it out for you. I'll keep two lovely plaits, just to please you.'

He looked at her again in the mirror.

'I'll cut it now. We'll shave it all off. Nobody will recognise you with a bald head.'

He closed his eyes. She picked up her electric razor, and with a few rapid movements she made Tharlo completely bald. His ponytail fell by his feet, still tied together by the red thread. He looked at it, picked it up and put it in his pocket.

That night she took him to the same bar they had been to before. They drank bottle after bottle of beer and had a wonderful time. It was very late when they went back to her place.

When Tharlo woke in the morning, the girl was nowhere to be seen. He looked around, and saw that his satchel was also gone.

He stayed in town looking for her. For two days and two nights he didn't stop searching, but there was no trace of her.

Two days later Tharlo went to the township police station. The police chief and a few other policemen were there busily working.

Tharlo greeted him, 'Chief, here I am.'

The police chief gave him a long and hard look, finally recognising him. 'Ponytail! What have you done to yourself? Where is your ponytail?'

'I had it cut off.'

'What a pity.'

'Chief, do you think I look like a bad person now?'

'What do you mean?'

'Isn't it true that you can tell a good person from a bad one with just a single glance?'

The police chief smiled. 'The only time you might have looked a little bit like a bad person was when you had your ponytail, but now you don't look anything at all like a bad person. You look like an absolutely good person.'

'I'm afraid my death will be lighter than a feather.'

The police chief was still smiling. 'So, do you want to recite the works of Chairman Mao again? I've heard what you can do with your memory trick. You don't have to repeat it.'

'It's such a pity. I can no longer die a death weightier than Mount Tai, just like Zhang Side did for the people. I can only die a death lighter than a feather, like those bad people who work for the fascists, and die for the exploiters and oppressors.'

The police chief smiled. 'This time you understand Chairman Mao better.'

Tharlo kept saying, 'What a shame!'

The police chief smiled. Then he turned to one of the other policemen. 'Hey, can you believe it? This young man can recite by heart many passages from the writings of Chairman Mao?'

They stopped what they were doing and looked at Tharlo sceptically, as if to say, 'Him?'

The police chief said, 'So, now we have to show you!'

He turned to Tharlo. 'Why not recite *Serve the People*. Show them!'

Tharlo looked at the expressions of the policemen. Without another word he started reciting, '*Serve the People*. Eighth of September, nineteen forty-four. Mao Zedong. Our Communist Party and the Eighth Route and New Fourth Armies led by our Party are battalions of our revolution. These battalions of ours are wholly dedicated to the liberation of the people and work entirely in the people's interests. Comrade Zhang Side was in the ranks of these battalions.

'All men must die, but death can vary in its significance. The ancient Chinese writer Sima Qian said: *Though death befalls all men alike, it may be weightier than Mount Tai or lighter than a feather*. To die for the people is weightier than Mount Tai, but to work for the fascists and die for the exploiters and oppressors is lighter than a feather. Comrade Zhang Side died for the people, and his death is indeed weightier than Mount Tai . . .'

The policemen looked at Tharlo and their jaws dropped in amazement.

The police chief signaled for Tharlo to stop, then he turned to the bemused policemen. 'So, what do you think? Unbelievable, isn't it? He can recite many other pieces from the works of Chairman Mao.'

They still had their eyes fixed on Tharlo, dumbfounded.

The police chief said, 'That's enough. Let's get to work. We're wasting time.'

Tharlo said, 'Mr Police Chief, I've become a bad person now.'

The police chief looked at him. 'You don't become a bad person just because you've shaved your head.'

Then he said to one of the policemen, 'Look in the new identity cards, and find his.'

The policeman asked, 'What's his name?'

The police chief said, 'Ponytail.'

The policeman responded in surprise, 'Really?'

The police chief corrected himself, 'No, that's his nickname.' Then he turned to Tharlo, 'What's your real name?'

Tharlo answered, 'Tharlo.'

The police chief said, 'Yes, now I remember. You're Tharlo.'

The policeman continued to search for Tharlo's card in the filing cabinet.

After a few more minutes he came over with the card. 'Chief, is this him? Now the photo doesn't look anything like him.'

The police chief took a good look at the card. Then he turned to Tharlo.

'Are you planning to grow a ponytail again?'

'No.'

'Then you've got to go back and get a new photo. This photo doesn't look like you. People who see your identity card won't be able to tell it's the same person.'

Tharlo was on the point of saying something, when the police chief interrupted, 'Go and come back as soon as you have the photo. We're very busy today.'

ༀ་གཟིན་ཞྭ་ལ་དར་པའེར། རྗེ་སྙེ། བོ་གྱུག ཝར་གར་ཕོགས་ལ་ཚང་དྲར་ཕོ་ཚོག

We can go to Lhasa, Beijing, Shanghai,
Guangzhou and Hong Kong.
Anywhere.

ཤིན་ཏུ་ཞེས་བསྐུལ་ན་ང་ལ་ཨེ་རུང་ཞིག་དང་འགྲུལ་བ།

Do you think I look like a bad person now?

>> The Script & The Film

The Script[1]

Scene 1   **Village committee office. Interior. Day.**

Close-up on a camera.

A man's voice is heard from the position of the camera. It sounds as if it is coming from the camera. The voice calls out villagers' names. They answer him as VO. Sounds of the camera clicking are heard as the villagers answer his calls. (Humorous lines to be improvised by actors during the shoot.)

Cut to a white fabric background placed opposite the camera in the film narrative.

The voice calls out a man's name. A man's face comes into the frame to form a portrait view exactly like a passport photo. He looks stiff, and uses his fingers to gently brush back his hair.

Voice: Ready. Please don't move. *The man moves his head slightly.*

Voice: Just keep still. Your clothes won't show. *The man keeps still. He moves the corner of his mouth to give the expression of something resembling a smile.*

On one side is a desk. Behind the desk is a policeman. On the desk is a notebook computer. The man's face is seen on the computer screen. The face has an expression that resembles a smile.

The policeman says to the man: Wipe that grin off your face. Be serious. This photo will be used on your identity card. You'll carry it for the rest of your life.

---

[1]   Rather than editing the shooting script into a format complying with the convention of a script, the original format showing the prosaic traits of its adaptive origin from the short story is retained. Comparison with the film version is encouraged, not only in terms of scene arrangement, but also of the respective stages the two versions have arrived at in the process of adaptation from a linguistic to a visual conception of the narrative.

Cast and Crew

Director	Pema Tseden
Screenplay	Pema Tseden
Cast	Shide Nyima; Yangshik Tso
Production supervisor	Zhang Xianmin
Producers	Wu Leilei; Sean Wang
Cinematographer	Lu Songye
Sound director	Dukar Tserang
Production designer	Daktse Dundrup
Music	Wang Jue
Editing supervisor	Liao Ching-sung
Editor	Song Bing
Genre	Drama
Language	Tibetan (with English and Chinese subtitles)
Release	2015
Length	123 minutes
Presenter	Luo Fang
Co-presenters	Xu Li; Sun Jialin; Gong Yu; Qian Shimu
Production companies	Heaven Pictures (Beijing) Culture & Media Co. Ltd.; Beijing Ocean & Time Culture Communication Co. Ltd.; Beijing YiHe Star Film Production Ltd.
Co-production companies	iQIYI Motion Pictures (Beijing) Co. Ltd.; Beijing Taihe Entertainment Co. Ltd.

The man's face turns serious. The sound of the camera clicking.

Policeman: It's done. You can go.

The man seems to regret that it is over. So quick?

Policeman: Yes, it's done. It only takes seconds to shoot a photo.

Man: But isn't this still too quick?

Policeman: Just go. Don't waste time.

After a pause, the voice from the camera is heard again. Next, Li Maojia.

The man's face exits the frame. A middle-aged woman's face comes into the frame.

Frontal portrait view of the woman like a passport photo. She looks serious, and is wearing a pair of gold earrings.

Policeman: Please take off your earrings. No earrings in identity card photos. *The woman doesn't say anything. She takes off her earrings. The camera clicks again.*

Voice from camera: Done. Go.

Sounds of various people talking loudly. It creates the feeling of a bustling communal life. (A good number of villagers to take photos. Adjustments to be made on location. Details about some old people and young children to be added.)

The village committee office is smoky and stuffy. The photo-shooting area is empty. Many people of all ages are sitting around. A few village cadres and three policemen from the township police station are sitting at the desk in the front row facing the photo-shooting area. A policeman is looking at a name list, then calls out a name: Lhakar Yak.

No answer.

He calls again: Lhakar Yak!

In the crowd is a man dozing off. Another man sitting next to him pats him on the shoulder to wake him, and says: You didn't sleep well last night, did you? Up to no good, eh?

List of Prizes

Entry in *Orizzonte* section
The 72nd *La Biennale di Venezia* 2015

Best Adapted Screenplay
The 52nd Taipei Golden Horse Film Festival 2015

Achievement in Cinematography (Special Mention Winner)
The 9th Asia Pacific Screen Awards 2015

Best Performance by an Actor
The 9th Asia Pacific Screen Awards 2015

Best Film
The 5th *Festival de Cine La Orquidea Cuenca* 2015

Grand Prize
The 16th TOKYO FiLMeX 2015

Student Jury Prize
The 16th TOKYO FiLMeX 2015

Best Feature Film
The 12th Chinese Independent Film Festival 2015

Best New Male Actor
The 24th Shanghai Film Critics Award 2015

Winner of *Cyclo d'or* (Grand Prize)
The 22nd *Festival international des cinémas d'Asie de Vesoul* 2016

Winner of INALCO (*Institut national des langues et civilisations orientales*) Jury Award
The 22nd *Festival international des cinémas d'Asie de Vesoul* 2016

Best Director
The 22nd *Film Festival della Lessinia* 2016

Best Film (Drama)
The 1st *Mostra cinematografica cinese in Italia* 2016

NETPAC (Network for the Promotion of Asia Pacific Cinema) Award,
The 10th Five Flavours Film Festival of Warsaw 2016

Director of the Year
The *Youth Film Handbook* Awards for Excellence in Chinese-language Films 2016

Actress of the Year
The *Youth Film Handbook* Awards for Excellence in Chinese-language Films 2016

People around laugh. Lhakar Yak looks embarrassed. The man sitting next to him tells him: The police chief just called your name. *Lhakar Yak stands up. He looks at the police chief and the village chief.*

The village chief is slightly annoyed. He stares at him. Don't waste time. Come over to have your photo taken. *Lhakar Yak walks across, and sits down on a stool in front of the white background.*

The police chief clears his throat and says: Can you cut down on your smoking please? I'm having a cold. My throat is hurting. *The crowd don't seem to hear him. They continue smoking. Lhakar Yak looks at the police chief. The police chief shakes his head.*

Photographer: Look this way. This way. *Lhakar Yak looks to the direction of the camera, and grows nervous.*

Close-up on the camera.

Photographer 's voice: Be serious. Look more serious. Don't smile.

Close-up on Lhakar Yak. Exactly the same dimension as a passport photo.

Lhakar Yak adjusts his expression. He is wearing an amulet around his neck.

Policeman: Please take off your amulet. You can't wear it in your identity card photo. *Lhakar Yak doesn't say anything. He takes his amulet off. The clicking sound of the camera.*

Photographer 's voice: Done. You can go.

Still in close-up. Lhakar Yak turns to one side. Is my wife's name there?

Wide shot. The village chief smiles. Your wife's residential registration is yet to be transferred here. How could she be on our list?

Some in the crowd laugh. Someone says: I'm afraid they're yet to get married properly! *Some in the crowd laugh again.*

The police chief turns to Lhakar Yak: Is it true? How much longer are you going to delay your marriage certificate application?

Lhakar Yak: No more delay. No more. I'll get it done. I will.

The village chief laughs. Your child is already born. How much longer do you want to wait?

The police chief turns serious. Is that true? You must get your marriage certificate. Otherwise, you are breaking the law. We might even fine you.

Lhakar Yak: I see, I see. I'll get the marriage certificate done as soon as my identity card is done.

Village chief: Mr Police Chief, haven't we already got an identity card? Why are we getting a new one? Isn't it just a ploy to get money from ordinary folks like us?

The police chief grows very serious. You mustn't say things like this! Whatever we do, we do to serve the people. We serve the people. The current identity cards are far from perfect. Some bad people have taken others' cards, and done many bad things with them. We're now making you second generation identity cards. They are very different. You are the only person who can use your card. No one else can use it. Even if bad people get hold of it, they can't do anything bad with it.

The village chief thinks for a moment. Now you've explained it. In such case we must get new ones.

Police chief: I'm glad you understand.

The police chief calls another name. A middle-aged man comes over to have his photo taken. Then he presents an identity card to the police chief and the village chief. Can you change my father's card, too? He said this was too old. He wants a new one.

The police chief takes the card, and looks at it. This is a permanent one. It can't be changed.

Middle-aged man: Please get him a new one if you can.

Police chief: It really isn't necessary. *The middle-aged man walks away, not exactly happily. The police chief calls another name.*

A young man's face appears in front of the white background. The clicking sound of the camera. The young man's face exits the frame.

Police chief's voice: Tharlo.

The film title on the white background: Tharlo

No answer from the crowd. Sound of the pages of the name register being flipped through.

After a while the police chief's voice again: Tharlo. This is the last one. *No answer from the crowd.*

The police chief raises his voice: Quiet! Tharlo! Tharlo! *Still, no answer.*

Police chief: Tharlo! Is Tharlo here? *The police chief looks at the village chief next to him, and calls Tharlo's name again. The village chief looks equally puzzled.*

Police chief: Is there anyone named Tharlo here?

The village chief gives it some thought and says: It's unlikely we have anyone by that name here.

The police chief says with a stern face: I'm not asking whether it's likely. You have to tell me definitively whether such a person lives here.

The village chief racks his brains but can't recall anyone by that name. He finally says: Our village has hundreds of inhabitants. I can't remember everyone.

The police chief looks at him and asks: Then how can you manage as their village chief?

The villagers laugh. The village chief becomes annoyed. So he says to the police chief: The job of a village chief isn't to remember everyone's name. My job is to bring the entire village 'out of poverty onto the road of prosperity'. After all, I serve the people like you do.

The police chief looks at the village chief smilingly. The village chief continues: These women in our village keep pumping out babies. They don't care about the fine. We're talking about five or six births in just the last couple of days. How can I remember all of their names? Some of them don't even have names yet.

The police chief smiles. You're the village chief. You should remember everyone's name.

The village chief gives the police chief a stern look. Do you remember the names of everyone registered in your police station?

Police chief: That's a different matter. You're the chief of your village.

Village chief: And you're the chief of your police station.

The police chief smiles. If you don't know this person, I'll delete him from the list. But, if ever he finds himself denied accommodation in town, don't blame me.

The village chief smiles. He signals the village bookkeeper to come over and asks him: Is there a Tharlo in our village?

The bookkeeper is a middle-aged man. He gives it some thought, but can't recall anyone by that name. He looks at the village chief and the police chief, both waiting for him to answer. So he calls out the name of the chief of their production team: Dorje.

Dorje seems preoccupied with the thoughts of other things. He suddenly hears his name being called, he says: What is it?

The village chief and the police chief laugh. The bookkeeper asks Dorje the chief of production team: Look, you're sitting there but hear nothing. Your mind must have sneaked out for lunch! Do you know anyone named Tharlo in our village?

Dorje the chief of production team gives it some serious thought. Then he laughs. Yes, of course, you mean Ponytail!

The village chief and the bookkeeper join in his delight. Yes, of course. Ponytail. That's right. Tharlo is Ponytail, and Ponytail is Tharlo. The same person. We'd nearly forgotten about him.

The police chief looks at them, slightly puzzled. The village chief explains to him: 'Ponytail' is Tharlo's nickname. We all call him by his nickname, and have simply forgotten his real name!

The police chief asks: Where is he now? Why isn't he here to do his second generation identity card?

The village chief smiles. I'm afraid he hasn't even got his first generation identity card.

The police chief looks at the village chief, still puzzled. The village chief tells him: He grew up an orphan. No one could care for him. So, years ago

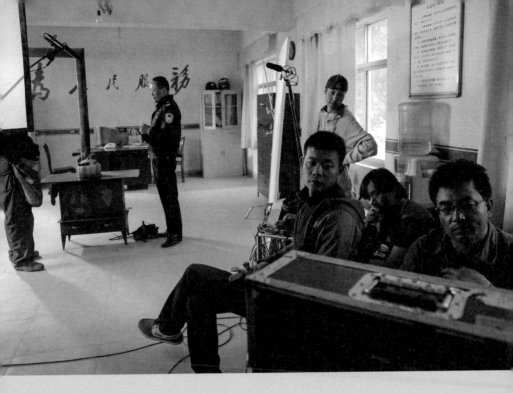

he took on the job of herding sheep in the mountains for families in the village. They pay him for that. Since then he's been living by himself in the mountains.

Police chief: Who gave him the nickname?

Village chief: I have no idea, but that's what everyone has called him since he was a teenager.

Police chief: As a member of the civic society, he can't do without an identity card. He must get it done this time. And he must come in person to get his photo taken. You have to go and get him.

Village chief: Must the photo be done today?

Police chief: Not today. But ask him to come to the township police station in a couple of days' time.

Village chief: In that case I'll look into getting him down from the mountains, and come to see you in town.

Scene 2   **On the road. Exterior. Morning.**

Day has just broken. Tharlo is riding a motorbike on a road. Back view. His face can't be seen. His ponytail is bouncing about.

Scene 3   **Township police station. Interior. Day.**

Written in paint in the most eye-catching manner on the frontal facing wall is the slogan 'Serve the People'. On both sides of it are print-outs of instructions and codes of all kinds posted on the wall. The police chief sits at his desk facing the door with his back to the slogan 'Serve the People'. He is reading a document.

A knock at the door is heard. It's a quiet knock. The police chief doesn't hear it.

After a while the knock is heard again. It is much louder this time. The police chief looks towards the door and says: Come in. *The door opens. Half of a man's head comes into the frame.*

Police chief: Can I help you?

The voice of that half-head: Is this the police station?

Police chief: Yes, it is.

Half a head: Can I see Chief Dorje, please?

Police chief: Come in first. We can talk in here.

The half of a man's head moves further into the frame to become a whole body.

This man is Tharlo. He enters the office and stands there, and looks at the police chief. He looks a bit nervous. He has a ponytail tied together with a red thread. On his shoulder is a satchel. He asks as soon as he comes in: Are you Chief Dorje?

Police chief: Yes, I am.

Tharlo looks at him, and then looks around. But you're alone in your office today.

The police chief smiles. Yes. The others are out on a case. I'm alone here today.

Tharlo responds with a 'right'. Then he says: Our village chief has sent me here to get my photo taken for the identity card.

The police chief looks at Tharlo closely. That makes him more nervous. So he lowers his head. Now the police chief can see his ponytail.

Police chief: Turn slightly to one side. *Tharlo turns slightly to one side.*

The police chief sees the hair tied up with a red thread. He laughs. Are you Ponytail?

Tharlo is surprised. He looks at the police chief and says: How did you know?

The police chief smiles. We policemen naturally know more than other people.

With a touch of admiration, Tharlo says: No wonder, you've been able to catch some of the bad people.

The police chief laughs. Do you mean that there are some bad people we haven't caught?

Tharlo: That's right. Last year I had three ewes and nine lambs stolen. You didn't manage to catch that thief.

Police chief: Did you report the theft?

Tharlo: Of course I did. I asked the village chief to do it for me.

Police chief: He's a busy man. Perhaps he forgot.

Tharlo: Maybe. But later on I asked him, and he swore to me he had been here to report it.

Police chief: There are lots of incidents like that. Losing a few sheep here and there.

Tharlo: On the other hand, the year before last a thief stole twelve of my sheep, and you caught him just one month later. You really are good.

The police chief can't help laughing and says: When you lose that many at one time, obviously we have to do something.

Tharlo: I see. *The police chief laughs, and looks at Tharlo.*

The sound of a lamb bleating is heard coming from Tharlo's general direction. The police chief looks up and down at him curiously. Tharlo turns his satchel to the front. A little lamb has popped its head outside the satchel. It is still bleating. Tharlo takes the lamb out. Then he takes a milk bottle out, also from the satchel, to feed it. The lamb goes quiet. Tharlo looks at the police chief and smiles.

Police chief: Why do you take the lamb around with you? Where is the mother?

Tharlo says with a touch of sadness: Its mother was killed by a wolf a month ago. Other ewes won't take care of it. So I have to.

The police chief looks at Tharlo. You have a good heart.

Now the lamb is being fed, and goes very quiet. Tharlo puts it back in the satchel. The police chief looks at him and smiles.

Tharlo looks at him in admiration. Honestly, the year before last you caught the thief who stole twelve of my sheep just one month later. You really are good.

Still smiling, the police chief responds to Tharlo's earlier admiration with an air of humility as he looks at the slogan on the wall. We serve the people.

Tharlo smiles, too. And he also looks at the slogan on the wall. I know that saying. Chairman Mao said that. I learnt it in school.

The police chief looks at Tharlo, as though now seeing him in a fresh light. You went to school?

Tharlo looks quite serious. Of course I went to school. I went to primary school and my grades were good. I learnt 'Serve the People' by heart.

Police chief: Did you? Do you still remember it?

Tharlo: Of course I do. I remember everything I've learned. I don't forget a thing.

Police chief: Do you know it in Chinese, or in Tibetan?

Tharlo: In Chinese.

Police chief: Well, then, why don't you recite it for me?

Tharlo thinks about it for a moment, then starts reciting, without having to pause (in Chinese with a heavy Qinghai dialectal accent): 'Serve The People'. Eighth of September, nineteen forty-four. Mao Zedong. Our Communist Party and the Eighth Route and New Fourth Armies led by our Party are battalions of our revolution. These battalions of ours are wholly dedicated to the liberation of the people and work entirely in the people's interests. Comrade Zhang Side was in the ranks of these battalions.

All men must die, but death can vary in its significance. The ancient Chinese writer Sima Qian said, 'Though death befalls all men alike, it may be weightier than Mount Tai or lighter than a feather.' To die for the people is weightier than Mount Tai, but to work for the fascists and die for the exploiters and oppressors is lighter than a feather. Comrade Zhang Side died for the people, and his death is indeed weightier than Mount Tai.

If we have shortcomings, we are not afraid to have them pointed out and criticised, because we serve the people. Anyone, no matter who, may point out our shortcomings. If he is right, we will correct them. If what

The Film

Scene 1 Police station. Interior. Day.

[Before picture fades in, Tharlo's voice is heard: Serve the people.*]*

Shot 1 *Close-up of a little lamb in a satchel popping its head out and sucking hard at the teat of a milk bottle. The hand that feeds the lamb is seen holding the bottle.*

Tharlo's voice: *[chanting in the style of traditional prayer]* Eighth of September, nineteen forty-four. Mao Zedong. Our Communist Party and the Eighth Route and New Fourth Armies led by our Party are battalions of our revolution. These battalions of ours are wholly dedicated to the liberation of the people and work entirely in the people's interests. Comrade Zhang Side was in the ranks of these battalions.

Shot 2 *Medium shot of Tharlo. Full frontal view.*

[Tharlo stands in front of a tall stove pipe with a sharp 90 degree angle. In the background on the frontal facing wall is written in paint in the most eye-catching manner the slogan 'Serve the people'. A desk and two chairs can be seen in front of the wall. On Tharlo's shoulder is the strap of his satchel with the lamb inside.]

Tharlo: *[reciting in the tone of religious chant without having to pause and think]* All men must die, but death can vary in its significance. The ancient Chinese writer Sima Qian said, 'Though death befalls all men alike, it may be weightier than Mount Tai or lighter than a feather.' To die for the people is weightier than Mount Tai, but to work for the fascists and die for the exploiters and oppressors is lighter than a feather. Comrade Zhang Side died for the people, and his death is indeed weightier than Mount Tai.

If we have shortcomings, we are not afraid to have them pointed out and criticised, because we serve the people. Anyone, no matter who, may point out our shortcomings. If he is right, we will correct them. If what he proposes will benefit the people, we will act upon it. The idea of 'better troops and simpler administration' was put forward by Mr Li Dingming, who is not a Communist. He made a good suggestion which is of benefit to the people, and we have adopted it. If, in the interests of the people, we persist in doing what is right and correct what is wrong, our ranks will surely thrive.

We hail from all corners of the country and have joined together for a common revolutionary objective. And we need the vast majority of a people with us on the road to this objective. Today, we already lead base areas with a population of ninety-one million, but this is not enough; to liberate the whole nation more are needed. In times of difficulty we must not lose sight of our achievements, must see the bright future and must pluck up courage. The Chinese people are suffering; it is our duty to serve them and we must exert ourselves in the struggle. Wherever there is struggle there is sacrifice, and death is a common occurrence. But we have the interests of the people and the sufferings of the great majority at heart, and when we die for the people it is a worthy death. Nevertheless, we should do our best to avoid unnecessary sacrifices. Our cadres must show concern for every soldier, and all people in the revolutionary ranks must care for each other, must love and help each other.

From now on, when anyone in our ranks who has done some useful work dies, be he soldier or cook, we should have a funeral ceremony and a memorial meeting in his honour. This should become the rule. And it should be introduced among the people as well. When someone dies in a village, let a memorial meeting be held. In this way we express our mourning for the dead and unite all the people. *(The entire recitation is completed in one shot.)*

When he finishes, the police chief is staring at him open-mouthed. Tharlo asks: How was it? Did I make any mistakes?

Only then is the police chief able to recover and resume his normal expression. I didn't know you were a genius!

Tharlo doesn't think he is, so he says: I just have a slightly better memory than other people.

he proposes will benefit the people, we will act upon it. The idea of 'better troops and simpler administration' was put forward by Mr Li Dingming, who is not a Communist. He made a good suggestion which is of benefit to the people, and we have adopted it. If, in the interests of the people, we persist in doing what is right and correct what is wrong, our ranks will surely thrive.

We hail from all corners of the country and have joined together for a common revolutionary objective. And we need the vast majority of a people with us on the road to this objective. Today, we already lead base areas with a population of ninety-one million, but this is not enough; to liberate the whole nation more are needed. In times of difficulty we must not lose sight of our achievements, must see the bright future and must pluck up courage. The Chinese people are suffering; it is our duty to serve them and we must exert ourselves in the struggle. Wherever there is struggle there is sacrifice, and death is a common occurrence. But we have the interests of the people and the sufferings of the great majority at heart, and when we die for the people it is a worthy death. Nevertheless, we should do our best to avoid unnecessary sacrifices. Our cadres must show concern for every soldier, and all people in the revolutionary ranks must care for each other, must love and help each other.

From now on, when anyone in our ranks who has done some useful work dies, be he soldier or cook, we should have a funeral ceremony and a memorial meeting in his honour. This should become the rule. And it should be introduced among the people as well. When someone dies in a village, let a memorial meeting be held. In this way we express our mourning for the dead and unite all the people.

[Tharlo slightly turns his body to one side to break the static frontal formation as he addresses his question to his interlocutor.]

Tharlo: How was it? Did I make any mistakes?

Police chief: You have an excellent memory.

[The police chief enters the frame as he speaks and walks past Tharlo on the right hand side in the picture. He is walking towards his desk placed by the frontal wall with the slogan in the deep area of the scene.]

Tharlo: *[He doesn't think he has an excellent memory.]* I just have a slightly better memory than other people.

Police chief: When did you learn this?

Tharlo: About nine years old. Back then all the texts in our books were taken from the works of Chairman Mao. I can recite many other works by him.

Police chief: You really are clever. How old are you?

Tharlo: I can't remember. Past forty, I think.

Police chief: You have such a remarkable memory. Why can't you remember your own age?

Tharlo: No one ever reminds me. And I hardly pay any attention to this kind of thing.

Police chief: It doesn't matter. We have it in our record. We'll know when we get your identity card.

The police chief murmurs a few more words of praise for Tharlo, and says: If I had a memory like yours, I would have gone to university.

Tharlo: I stopped after primary school. My parents died young. My relatives didn't want to take care of me. They said that I had a good memory, and that I should look after sheep for a few households and herd them in the mountain. They also told me I only needed to remember the colour and markings of each sheep. If I didn't lose any sheep, I could make a living at it. There were no other openings for me, so I took the sheep to the mountains. I started with one hundred and thirty-six. The second year I had sixteen more. The third year I had forty-seven more. The fourth year I had only eleven more. That year we had a bad snowstorm. It killed many lambs. In any case, every year I have more sheep. There hasn't been a single year that I've had fewer. Now I have as many as three hundred seventy-five; of them two hundred and nine are white, seventy-one black, ninety-five mixed. One hundred thirty-four have horns, two hundred forty-one don't.

Again, the police chief is amazed. After regaining his composure, he says: What a waste! What a waste! This is such a waste of someone like you!

Tharlo says, with a touch of pride: The way I think about it is that I'm also serving the people by herding their sheep, although they pay me about a dozen sheep every year, and also some money.

[*Tharlo continues to turn to face the police chief, establishing a sideview of the two characters standing face to face talking to each other. Now Tharlo is under the right angle formed by the stove pipe, creating the mise-en-abîme effect of him inside a picture or mirror frame.*]

Police chief: When did you learn this?

Tharlo: When I was about nine years old. Back then all the texts in our books were taken from the works of Chairman Mao. I can recite many other works by him.

Police chief: You really are clever. How old are you?

Tharlo: I can't remember. Past forty, I think.

Police chief: You have such a remarkable memory. Why can't you remember your own age?

Tharlo: No one ever reminds me. And I hardly pay any attention to this kind of thing. Honestly, I don't know how old I am.

Police chief: It doesn't matter. We have it in our record. We'll know when we get your identity card.

Police chief: [*murmuring a few more words of praise*] Well, you do have a good memory. If I had a memory like yours, I would have gone to university.

Tharlo: I stopped after primary school. My parents died young. My relatives didn't want to take care of me. They said that I had a good memory, and that I should look after sheep for a few households and herd them in the mountain. They also told me I only needed to remember the colour and markings of each sheep. If I didn't lose any sheep to wolves, I could make a living at it. There were no other openings for me, so I took the sheep to the mountains. I started with one hundred and thirty-six. The second year I had sixteen more. The third year I had forty-seven more. The fourth year I had only eleven more. That year we had a bad snowstorm. It killed many lambs. In any case, every year I have more sheep. There hasn't been a single year that I've had fewer. Now I have as many as three hundred and seventy-five; of them two hundred and nine are white, seventy-one black, ninety-five mixed. One hundred thirty-four have horns, two hundred forty-one don't.

The police chief is quick to nod his head in agreement. Yes, of course, of course.

Tharlo: If you don't catch any thieves, do you still get your salary from the government?

Police chief: Of course we do. Otherwise, how do we raise our family?

Tharlo wishes he was in the same position. Not bad for you.

Police chief: No one is doing better or worse. We all serve the people.

Tharlo seems to have forgotten what they are talking about. He digresses: I like what Chairman Mao said about death, 'Though death befalls all men alike, it may be weightier than Mount Tai or lighter than a feather.'

The police chief resumes his normal expression. Look, you certainly have remembered the piece accurately, but you haven't really understood it, have you? Chairman Mao didn't say that, Sima Qian said that. Sima Qian was a great writer.

Tharlo: Is that so? How were Chairman Mao and Sima Qian related?

The police chief laughs. They weren't related. Sima Qian lived in ancient times. Chairman Mao lived in modern times. There wasn't much of a relationship between them.

Tharlo doesn't quite understand, and asks him: Then what about this part: 'To die for the people is weightier than Mount Tai, but to work for the fascists and die for the exploiters and oppressors is lighter than a feather. Comrade Zhang Side died for the people, and his death is indeed weightier than Mount Tai'? Chairman Mao did say that, didn't he?

Police chief: Yes, that he did say.

Tharlo: How come they talked so alike?

Police chief: They both meant the same thing.

Tharlo: I herd sheep for people in our village. Will my death be weightier than Mount Tai like Zhang Side's?

Police chief: Yes, definitely. Your death will certainly be weightier than Mount Tai, like Zhang Side's, but don't worry, that's still a long way off. In any case I can tell you are a good person, a good person like Zhang Side.

Police chief: *[amazed, then regaining his composure]* What a waste! What a waste! This is such a waste of someone like you!

Tharlo: *[with a touch of pride]* The way I think about it is that I'm also serving the people by herding their sheep, although they pay me about a dozen sheep every year, and also some money.

Police chief: You work so hard tending their sheep. Of course they should pay you.

Tharlo: Chief Dorje, if you don't catch any thieves, do you still get your salary from the government?

Police chief: Of course we do. Otherwise, how do we raise our family?

Tharlo: *[wishing he was in the same position]* Not bad for you.

Police chief: No one is doing better or worse. We all serve the people.

Tharlo: *[seeming to have forgotten what they are talking about, and digressing]* I like what Chairman Mao said about death, 'Though death befalls all men alike, it may be weightier than Mount Tai or lighter than a feather.'

Police chief: *[resuming his normal expression]* Look, you certainly have remembered the piece accurately, but you haven't really understood it, have you? Chairman Mao didn't say that, Sima Qian said that. Sima Qian was a great writer.

Tharlo: Is that so? How were Chairman Mao and Sima Qian related?

Police chief: *[laughing]* They weren't related. Sima Qian lived in ancient times. Chairman Mao lived in modern times. There wasn't much of a relationship between them.

Tharlo: *[not quite understanding]* Then what about this part: 'To die for the people is weightier than Mount Tai, but to work for the fascists and die for the exploiters and oppressors is lighter than a feather. Comrade Zhang Side died for the people, and his death is indeed weightier than Mount Tai'? Chairman Mao did say that, didn't he?

Police chief: Yes, that he did say.

Tharlo: How come they talked so alike?

Tharlo: How can you tell I'm a good person like Zhang Side?

Police chief: We can tell good people from bad with a single glance. We policemen might not be experts in everything, but when it comes to that, we know what we're doing.

Tharlo: Can you explain to me how you tell good people from bad?

The police chief gives him a mysterious smile. This I can't tell you. It's how we earn our keep.

Tharlo is slightly disappointed. But, at the same time, he can't hide the admiration in his eyes.

The police chief repeats his praise. You certainly have a good memory!

Tharlo suddenly remembers why he has come, and says: I've come to have a photograph taken. Our village chief sent me here.

The police chief looks askance, and gives him a harsh look from the corner of his eye. Why has it taken you so long? It's been quite a few days. Now you've got to go to the township to get it taken.

Tharlo: Our village chief found someone to stand in for me only yesterday. I came as soon as I could.

Police chief: Now you'll have to go to the township to do it.

Tharlo: Must I have it done?

Police chief: Yes, you must. It's for your identity card.

Tharlo: What's an identity card?

Police chief: Now I remember. Your village chief said you hadn't even got the first generation identity card. Am I right?

Tharlo: No, I haven't. I haven't got anything. I've just come like this.

Police chief: This time you must do it.

Tharlo: Must I really?

Police chief: When you go into town, people will know who you are by looking at your identity card. Otherwise, people won't know who you are.

Police chief: They both meant the same thing.

Tharlo: I herd sheep for people in our village. Will my death be weightier than Mount Tai like Zhang Side's?

Police chief: Yes, definitely. Your death will certainly be weightier than Mount Tai, like Zhang Side's, but don't worry, that's still a long way off. In any case I can tell you are a good person, a good person like Zhang Side.

Tharlo: How can you tell I'm a good person like Zhang Side?

Police chief: We can tell good people from bad with a single glance. We policemen might not be experts in everything, but when it comes to that, we know what we're doing.

Tharlo: Can you explain to me how you tell good people from bad?

Police chief: [smiling mysteriously] This I can't tell you. It's how we earn our keep.

[Tharlo is slightly disappointed. But, at the same time, he can't hide the admiration in his eyes.]

Police chief: [repeating his praise] You certainly have a good memory!

Tharlo: [suddenly remembering why he has come] I've come to have a photograph taken. Our village chief sent me here.

Police chief: Why has it taken you so long? It's been quite a few days. Now you've got to go to the township to get it taken.

[As the police chief says this, he goes to sit at his desk placed at the deep area of the scene. Tharlo turns to face him, still standing. Now he has his back to the camera. His face is no longer seen, but his ponytail is seen in full view. Throughout the following conversation the camera remains focused on Tharlo's position under the stove pipe. It continues to focus on the same spot after he moves away. This cinematographic style recurs throughout the film.]

Tharlo: Our village chief only found someone to stand in for me yesterday. I came as soon as I could.

Police chief: Now you'll have to go to the township to do it.

Tharlo: Isn't it enough that I know who I am?

The police chief smiles. What is your name?

Tharlo: Ponytail.

Police chief: No, your real name.

Tharlo thinks about it for a moment. Tharlo.

Police chief: Tharlo, yes. Go into town today. Look for Dekyi Photo Studio. That is our designated studio for the identity card. The owner there is called Dekyi. Say that you have been sent to her by the police for a photo. She'll know what to do.

Tharlo smiles. This real name of mine doesn't feel like mine at all. It sounds strange even to my own ears.

The police chief looks at the watch on his wrist. Don't waste your time talking. Go on.

Tharlo says: I see, I see. I'll go right now.

Police chief: How did you come? On horse-back?

Tharlo laughs. Who would ride a horse now? We don't have a single horse in the village. Now shepherds ride motorbikes. I came on my motorbike.

Police chief: You have a motorbike. Not bad at all.

Tharlo: I bought it second-hand from someone. It keeps breaking down.

Police chief: Go on. You'll get there in no time on a motorbike.

Tharlo: I see. I'll go now.

Tharlo leaves the office, and shuts the door from outside.

Tharlo: Must I have it done?

Police chief: Yes, you must. It's for your identity card.

Tharlo: What's an identity card?

Police chief: Now I remember. Your village chief said you hadn't even got the first generation identity card. Am I right?

Tharlo: No, I haven't. I haven't got anything. I've just come like this.

Police chief: This time you must do it.

Tharlo: Must I really?

Police chief: When you go into town, people will know who you are by looking at your identity card. Otherwise, people won't know who you are.

Tharlo: Isn't it enough that I know who I am?

Police chief: [smiling] What is your name?

Tharlo: Ponytail.

Police chief: No, your real name.

Tharlo: [thinking for a moment] Tharlo.

Police chief: Tharlo, yes. Go into town today. Look for Dekyi Photo Studio. That is our designated studio for the identity card. The owner there is called Dekyi. Say that you have been sent to her by the police for a photo. She'll know what to do.

Tharlo: [smiling] Tharlo... Tharlo...This real name of mine doesn't feel like mine at all. It sounds strange even to my own ears.

Police chief: [looking at the watch on his wrist] Don't waste your time talking. Go on.

Scene 4   **A road leading to the township. Exterior. Day.**

Tharlo is riding an old motorbike on a dirt road leading to town. His expression is serious. (Suggestion: Shooting on the runway of Chabcha Airport.) The motorbike is making a lot of noise, and going very fast. Other people on the road look on in surprise.

Scene 5   **Streets of the county town. Exterior. Day.**

Tharlo arrives at a crossroad on his motorbike. He stops on a roadside, and looks around. He feels slightly unsettled and nervous. He looks at the people rushing around and has no idea which way to go.

(Chinese dialogue in this scene.)

Tharlo sees a primary school child with a red scarf walking past. He stops him and asks: Little friend, do you know where Dekyi Photo Studio is?

The primary school child stares at him, then at his ponytail, and shakes his head vigorously as if he's afraid of Tharlo.

Tharlo: Little friend, don't be frightened. My name is Ponytail. I need to go to Dekyi Photo Studio to have a photo taken.

The school child is now amused. If you let me look at your ponytail, I'll take you there.

Tharlo squats down quite happily, so that the boy can have a look at his ponytail.

The boy shows great interest in Tharlo's ponytail. Our teacher said only people in the Manchurian dynasty wore ponytails. Why do you still have one?

Tharlo laughs. There's nothing strange about it. A few of us in our place have a ponytail.

Boy: I've never heard of men having a ponytail.

Tharlo gets up and smiles. Now, will you take me to Dekyi Photo Studio?

The boy suddenly grows nervous again. I don't remember exactly where it is.

Scene 2 **A road leading to the township. Exterior. Day.**

Shot 3 *Extreme wide shot. Tharlo is seen riding into the frame on his motorbike along a road with his back to the camera. At the end of the road are clusters of township buildings.*

Tharlo grows desperate. He takes out a ten-yuan note. Take me there and I'll give you this.

The boy looks pleased. Fine. I'll take you there. *Tharlo starts his motorbike.*

Boy: Do we go on this motorbike?

Tharlo: We can do.

The boy asks a passer-by the location of the studio. The passer-by points out its direction to the boy as he explains. The boy mounts the motorbike, and says to Tharlo: Straight on. Now I know. *After a while he says:* Here we are. Stop on the side. *He points to a shop a few steps away, and tells Tharlo:* That is Dekyi Photo Studio.

Tharlo looks toward that direction, and sees many photos in the window. He takes a ten-yuan note out from his pocket, and gives it to the boy. The boy clutches the ten-yuan note, and dashes into the adjacent snack shop.

Tharlo enters the photo studio.

Scene 6   Dekyi photo studio. Interior. Day.

Tharlo opens the door and enters. He sees a woman with a camera taking wedding photos of a couple. Tharlo stands there and watches.

The couple are wearing Tibetan robes standing in front of a backdrop printed with a photo of the Potala Palace. They look nervous. Dekyi asks the couple to hold each other's hand. They are too embarrassed to do so. With some difficulty the man overcomes the embarrassment and puts his arm around the woman's shoulder.

Dekyi: Good. Stay like that. Just stand there. Don't move. *The camera clicks.*

Dekyi: Done. Change the background.

Her assistant asks: What to?

Dekyi: What about Beijing Tian'anmen?

Assistant: Fine. *He changes the background.*

Scene 3   **Dekyi photo studio. Interior. Day.**

Shot 4   *Medium shot. Photographer in foreground adjusting the settings of her camera. Tharlo enters frame from the right in the background.*

Photographer: *[to her client in front of her - who is not seen in the frame]* Pay attention.

Tharlo: Is this Dekyi photo studio?

Photographer: *[turning to answer him]* Yes.

Tharlo: I'm here to see Dekyi.

Photographer: I'm Dekyi. Take a seat. I'll be with you shortly.

Tharlo: Alright. *[He sits down on a bench right behind him.]*

Dekyi asks the couple who are now standing on the side: How about Beijing Tian'anmen?

The man says: It's fine by us. You decide.

Dekyi: It looks good to me.

Man: That's good.

Dekyi asks the couple to stand in front of the backdrop. You must make sure that you are relaxed. The photo will look much better that way.

The couple stand in front of the backdrop. The camera clicks. Dekyi: Done.

Dekyi looks at the couple. The last one. Let's have New York in America.

Man: You decide. We don't know about these things.

Dekyi tells the assistant to change the backdrop. The assistant starts to do so. At last he gets to one showing a street scene with the Statue of Liberty in the distance.

Dekyi: Good. Now go in front of it.

The couple stand in front of the backdrop showing the New York street scene. They straighten their back, and look at Dekyi. Dekyi takes a good look at them. Let me see. You look awkward, but why?

The couple smile nervously, not knowing what to do. Dekyi laughs. That's it! It's your clothes. They don't go with the background. Why don't you change into something in Western style?

Man: We haven't brought any Western style clothes with us.

Dekyi: You don't have to. We've got some here for clients. Just put some on.

Dekyi points to the direction of her assistant: Follow him to the changing room, and get changed. *They follow him.*

Dekyi turns to ask Tharlo: Can I help you?

Tharlo asks her: Is this Dekyi Photo Studio?

Dekyi turns toward Tharlo. Yes, this is Dekyi Photo Studio. Can I help you?

Shot 5   *Full shot. A couple in Tibetan clothes sitting in front of a scenic backdrop of the Potala Palace. Full frontal view. They look nervous.*

Dekyi's voice: Good. Stay like that. Don't move.

[The camera clicks and lights flash.]

Dekyi's voice: Done. Change the background.

[The photographer's assistant enters the frame.]

Assistant: What to?

Dekyi's voice: What about Beijing Tian'anmen?

Assistant: Fine. *[He changes the background, then exits.]*

Dekyi's voice: How do you like Beijing Tian'anmen?

Man: Not bad.

Dekyi's voice: It looks good to me.

Man: It's fine by us if you like it.

Dekyi's voice: Don't be nervous. Just relax. Good, look here. Smile. Good. One, two, three. *[Lights flash.]* Done. This is a good one. Let's change the backdrop. Let's have the Statue of Liberty in New York of America.

[The assistant enters, changes the backdrop, then exits.]

Dekyi's voice: How do you like the Statue of Liberty of America?

Man: This looks nice. *[They straighten their back, and look at Dekyi.]*

Dekyi's voice: Let me see. You look awkward.

[The couple smile nervously, not knowing what to do.]

Dekyi's voice: You would look better in Western clothes.

Man: We haven't brought any Western clothes with us.

Dekyi's voice: *[to her assistant]* We've got some here for clients. Give them some Western clothes.

Tharlo: I'm here to see Dekyi.

She stops what she is doing and looks at Tharlo with suspicion. I'm Dekyi.

Tharlo gives her a smile. I've come to have a photo taken. Chief Dorje of our police station sent me here.

Dekyi: I see. Do you want a passport photo?

Tharlo: I don't know. He said it was for some sort of card.

Dekyi smiles. Why didn't you say so? That's a passport photo. It's for the identity card. The way you go on! I was wondering what you wanted. Take a seat. Wait a while. I'll take your photo as soon as I finish with them. I'm be fast.

Tharlo sits in the chair on one side as he says: Alright.

The couple come back in Western clothes. Dekyi looks at them and smiles. Not bad, not bad at all. Quick! Stand in front of the backdrop. *They stand in front of the backdrop, looking nervous.*

Dekyi: Now give each other a hug. Relax.

The couple have no idea what to do. Suddenly Tharlo's lamb bleats. Everybody looks towards him. Tharlo opens his satchel, and takes the lamb out.

Dekyi: Why are you carrying a lamb with you?

Tharlo: His mother was killed by a wolf. Other ewes won't take care of him. So I'm taking care of him.

Dekyi: You have a good heart.

Tharlo feeds the lamb with a milk bottle. Dekyi turns back to the couple and focuses on them. The couple are still nervous. The woman asks Tharlo: Can I hold your little lamb?

Tharlo looks at her, only very briefly. Of course. *He gives the lamb to her. She fixes her eyes on the lamb. Now she looks relaxed.*

Tharlo: His mother was killed by a wolf. He's an orphan now. You just got married. It isn't very lucky to be holding him in your wedding photo, is it?

[The assistant enters with some Western clothes for the couple. He points out to them the direction of the changing room. Then all three exit.]

Dekyi's voice: Can I help you?

Shot 6   *Medium shot. Tharlo's head near lower right-hand corner of the frame. There are some photos on the wall behind him.*

Tharlo: Chief Dorje sent me here.

Dekyi: I see. Do you want a passport photo?

Tharlo: I don't know. He said it was for some sort of card.

Dekyi: *[smiling]* That's a passport photo. It's for the identity card. You don't look like you've come to take a photo. Take a seat. Wait a while. I'll take your photo as soon as I finish with them. I'll be fast.

Tharlo: Alright.

Shot 7   *Full shot on the backdrop with the Statue of Liberty. Same composition as Shot 5.*

[The couple now in Western clothes enter frame, then sit down.]

Dekyi's voice: Don't move. Look here. Relax. You look nervous. You do look better in Western clothes.

[They straighten their jackets. Suddenly Tharlo's lamb bleats. Everybody looks towards him.]

Dekyi's voice: Why are you carrying a lamb with you?

Tharlo's voice: I carry it with me everywhere. I'm used to it. He's a good boy.

Woman: *[to Tharlo, still nervous]* Can I hold your little lamb?

Tharlo's voice: Of course.

[Tharlo enters frame from the right, and gives the lamb to her. She holds the lamb. Now she looks relaxed.]

Woman: You have a lovely little lamb.

Woman: It's fine. We also used to herd sheep.

Man: Exactly. It's fine. It really is fine.

Tharlo says nothing, and looks at them admiringly. The lamb keeps bleating in the woman's bosom. She strokes his head. The lamb doesn't stop. Tharlo goes over to the woman and gives her the milk bottle. She feeds the lamb, and the lamb goes quiet. The man also looks at the lamb and smiles.

Dekyi pushes Tharlo out of the way and presses the shuttle. Done. Your wedding photos are done. This one is excellent. You look so natural. I can put it in the window when it comes out.

Man: So quickly?

Dekyi: All done. Come back to pick up the photos later.

The woman gives the lamb back to Tharlo and smiles at him. Tharlo smiles back at her.

Dekyi: You can change your clothes back now.

Man: Yes. *They go to the changing room and get changed.*

Dekyi looks at Tharlo, and points to the direction of a white background. Sit over there. I'll take your photo now.

Tharlo puts the lamb back inside the satchel, and walks over to sit on a stool in front of the white backdrop.

Dekyi: Leave your satchel. No one carries a satchel in a photo. *She stands quite a distance away from Tharlo.*

Tharlo puts the satchel with the lamb inside on the floor to one side. He goes back to sit on the same stool, and tells Dekyi: Let's take it now.

All the lights are on Tharlo. He appears to glow.

Dekyi walks towards Tharlo with a camera, but suddenly stops to look at his ponytail as if discovering something new. She asks: Why are you wearing that ponytail?

Tharlo: I've had it since I was very young.

Tharlo: His mother was killed by a wolf. He's an orphan now. You just got married. It isn't very lucky to be holding him in your wedding photo, is it?

Woman: It's fine. We also used to herd sheep.

Man: Exactly. It's fine. It really is fine.

[Tharlo says nothing, and looks at them admiringly. Then he gives her the milk bottle. She feeds the lamb. Then the man takes the bottle, also to feed the lamb.]

Dekyi's voice: You look much more natural now. [to Tharlo] Go over to the side.

[Tharlo exits.]

Dekyi's voice: One, two, three!

[The camera clicks, and lights flash.]

Shot 8   Medium close-up on backdrop featuring a street scene of New York.

Dekyi's voice: Sit over there. I'll take your photo now.

Tharlo's voice: Alright.

[Tharlo walks into the frame and sits in front of the background.]

Dekyi's voice: Change the background to white.

[The background is changed to a white backdrop.]

Dekyi's voice: Leave your satchel. No one carries a satchel in a photo.

[Tharlo puts the satchel on the floor to one side.]

Dekyi's voice: Don't move. Look here. Take off your hat. [Tharlo takes his hat off.]

Dekyi's voice: Turn your head to one side. [Tharlo turns his head. She goes over to him to touch his ponytail, as if to make sure what it is.] Why are you wearing that ponytail?

Tharlo: I've kept it since I was very young.

Dekyi: You can't take your passport photo like that, can you?

Tharlo: Why not?

Dekyi: The police station won't be able to tell whether you're a man or a woman.

Tharlo grows very serious. I was just at the police station. Not even the police chief said anything.

Dekyi laughs. Well, that's fine. I'll just do the photo as you want. Sit up. Look this way.

Tharlo straightens his back like the people before him did. He is about to force a smile. Dekyi tries a few positions with her camera, then goes over and tries to tidy up his hair.

Dekyi walks back to her camera off screen. Dekyi's voice: I suggest you have your hair washed first. It's too messy now. The photo won't look good.

Tharlo: I'm not bothered.

Dekyi grows serious. You'll use this identity card for the rest of your life. Don't you want to look good in the photo?

Tharlo looks at Dekyi, hesitates, but says nothing. Dekyi points to a place outside the window. Tharlo sees a barbershop across the road. On its door is written in both Tibetan and Chinese, 'Auspicious Barbershop'.

Dekyi: Get your hair washed there. *Tharlo gets up, reluctantly.*

Tharlo is leaving the studio as Dekyi calls from behind him: Take your lamb with you. *Tharlo turns back, and picks up the satchel with the lamb inside. Then he leaves the studio.*

Scene 7   Barbershop. Interior. Day.

Tharlo is seen through the glass door. He opens the door of the barbershop and enters. A shorthaired girl is sitting on a single-seater sofa flipping through a magazine. She sees him and stands up.

[Dekyi walks back to her camera off screen.]

Dekyi's voice: I suggest you have your hair washed first. It's too messy now. The photo won't look good.

Scene 4   The street outside the photo studio. Exterior. Day.

Shot 9   Wide shot. Tharlo crosses the street with his back to the camera. The back of a truck occupies more than half of the frame. The following dialogue is heard as voice-over.

Tharlo's voice: I'm not bothered.

Dekyi's voice: You'll use this identity card for the rest of your life. Don't you want to look good in the photo?

Tharlo: I don't care.

Dekyi's voice: There is a barbershop on the other side of the street. Get your hair washed there.

Tharlo's voice: Alright.

[The truck drives off, revealing the sign of 'Yangtso Barbershop' on one of the shops on the opposite side of the street. Traffic noises are heard. Tharlo opens the door and enters the barbershop. The following dialogue is heard as voice-over.]

Female voice: Do you want a wet or dry wash?

Tharlo's voice: What do you mean by dry wash?

Female voice: That is a wash without using water.

Tharlo's voice: How do you wash something without water?

Female voice: It's nice. Try and you'll see.

Scene 5   Barbershop. Interior. Day.

Shot 10   Medium shot. Filmed as mirror reflection. Photos of trendy models are pasted on the wall. Tharlo is sitting in a barber's chair

The girl smiles. Please come in. Would you like your hair done?

Tharlo stands there feeling nervous, not quite knowing what to do. He looks at the shorthaired girl curiously. The photo studio opposite told me to get my hair washed here.

Shorthaired girl: Alright. Sit there please.

He takes the satchel off his shoulder, and leaves it on the sofa. The lamb starts bleating. The shorthaired girl grows curious and asks him: Why are you carrying a lamb with you?

Tharlo: His mother was killed by a wolf. Other ewes won't take care of him. So I have to.

Shorthaired girl: You are kind.

Tharlo smiles and says nothing. The shorthaired girl also smiles. He won't pee on my sofa, will he? I sleep there at night.

Tharlo looks at the lamb. I'll put him on the floor. *He puts the satchel on the floor. The lamb bleats.*

Shorthaired girl: Is he hungry?

Tharlo: No. I just fed him.

She looks at him again, and asks him to sit in a chair. She stands behind him, and looks at him in the mirror. Do you want a wet or dry wash? Five yuan for a wet wash, ten for a dry wash.

Tharlo looks back at her in the mirror. What do you mean by a dry wash? *She smiles as she replies:* That's washing without water.

Tharlo: How do you wash something without water?

Shorthaired girl: It's nice. Try it and you'll see.

Tharlo: Then I'll have a dry wash.

The shorthaired girl takes a shampoo cream and squeezes some onto his head, then starts gently rubbing it into his hair. From time to time she looks at Tharlo in the mirror. Tharlo also looks at her in the mirror. She looks back at him. The dry wash is nice, isn't it?

in front of the mirror. Very subtle flashing of fairy lights is seen at the corner of the frame. The hairdresser is a young woman with short hair. She is standing behind him, gently rubbing shampoo cream into his hair. From time to time Tharlo looks at her in the mirror.

Shorthaired girl: *[looking back at Tharlo in the mirror]* The dry wash is nice, isn't it?

Tharlo: It is.

Shorthaired girl: You haven't washed your hair for quite a while, have you?

Tharlo: I herd sheep. I don't have all that much water to wash my hair.

Shorthaired girl: *[putting on a deliberate look of surprise]* Oh, really?

Tharlo: It takes me over an hour to get there and back if I carry two plastic buckets to fetch water.

Shorthaired girl: How many sheep do you have?

Tharlo: *[without giving it a second thought]* I have three hundred and seventy-five in total, of them one hundred thirty-three are wethers, one hundred sixty-eight, ewes, seventy-four, half-grown lambs. Of the one hundred and sixty-eight ewes, one hundred and twenty-four will give lambs this year. Forty-four are too old to breed.

Shorthaired girl: You have a good memory!

Tharlo: *[not thinking much about his own memory]* I must remember everything about all of the sheep, so that I can take proper care of them.

Shorthaired girl: How much are all those sheep worth?

Tharlo: I sold two wethers on the way here today. They gave me one thousand two hundred yuan. Now it is about four hundred yuan for a ewe, probably a bit more if she is pregnant, around five hundred, maybe. And two hundred for a lamb. Altogether my sheep should be worth about one hundred and sixty or seventy thousand.

Shorthaired girl: That much?

Tharlo: It is.

She keeps rubbing Tharlo's hair. They are both quiet.

After a while she says: You haven't washed your hair for quite a while, have you?

Tharlo: I herd sheep. I don't have all that much water to wash my hair.

She puts on a deliberate look of surprise. Oh, really?

Tharlo: It takes me over an hour to get there and back if I carry two plastic buckets to fetch water.

Shorthaired girl: How many sheep do you have?

Tharlo says without giving it a second thought: I have three hundred seventy-five in total, of them one hundred thirty-three are wethers, one hundred sixty-eight, ewes, seventy-four, half-grown lambs. Of the one hundred sixty-eight ewes, one hundred twenty-four will give lambs this year. Forty-four are too old to breed.

She stops rubbing his hair and looks at him in amazement. You have a good memory!

Tharlo never thinks much about his own memory. I must remember everything about all of the sheep, so that I can take proper care of them.

She starts rubbing his hair again, still eying him in the mirror. How much are all those sheep worth?

Tharlo: I sold two wethers on the way here today. They gave me one thousand two hundred yuan. Now it is about four hundred yuan for a ewe, probably a bit more if she is pregnant, around five hundred, maybe. Altogether my sheep should be worth about one hundred and sixty or seventy thousand.

Her mouth opens slightly in surprise. That much?

Tharlo: But not all three hundred seventy-five sheep belong to me. Only about one hundred are mine.

Shorthaired girl: That's still quite a lot.

Tharlo: But not all three hundred seventy-five sheep belong to me. Only about one hundred are mine.

Shorthaired girl: That's still quite a lot.

[They are quiet for a while.]

Shorthaired girl: Isn't the dry wash nice?

Tharlo: Yes, very nice. That will do.

[She continues to massage his head for a while. From time to time they look at each other in the mirror. In a few instances their eyes meet.]

Tharlo: This should do now.

Shorthaired girl: *[smiling at him in the mirror]* Come over here. *[She takes him to sit under a tap to rinse his hair.]*

Tharlo: *[as she is rinsing his hair]* Didn't you say dry wash? Why are you using water?

Shorthaired girl: *[smiling]* The wash is dry, but the rinse requires water.

[Tharlo doesn't say anything, but lets her rinse his hair with water.]

Shorthaired girl: Is it hot?

Tharlo: A little, but it's fine.

[When she is done, she lets him sit back in the chair in front of the mirror, and starts drying his hair with an electric hair dryer. Tharlo stares at her in the mirror. She continues to dry his hair. Tharlo looks at her, and their eyes meet in the mirror. Tharlo dips his head. Then he stares at her in the mirror again.]

Shorthaired girl: What is your name?

Tharlo: Everyone calls me Ponytail.

Shorthaired girl: *[laughing]* That is your nickname, right? I mean your real name.

Tharlo: *[pause]* Tharlo.

Shorthaired girl: This is a nice name. Who gave you this name?

She takes him to sit under a tap to rinse his hair. Tharlo asks as she is rinsing his hair: Didn't you say dry wash? Why are you using water?

She smiles. The wash is dry, but the rinse requires water. *Tharlo doesn't say anything, but lets her rinse his hair with water.*

When she is done, she lets him sit back in the chair in front of the mirror, and starts drying his hair with an electric hair dryer. Tharlo stares at her in the mirror. She continues to dry his hair. Tharlo looks at her, and their eyes meet in the mirror. Tharlo dips his head. Then he stares at her in the mirror again.

She asks him: What is your name?

Tharlo: Everyone calls me Ponytail.

She laughs. That's your nickname, right? I mean your real name.

Tharlo pauses before he says, Tharlo.

Shorthaired girl: That's a nice name. Who gave you this name?

Tharlo: I don't know.

She laughs. Don't you know who gave you your name?

Tharlo stares at her in the mirror again. She smiles. Why are you looking at me like that? Do I look that good?

Tharlo keeps looking at her. I thought you were a man when I came in. Then I saw your earrings.

She gives a brief laugh. Short hair is trendy in the city. This is in fashion.

Tharlo: But how could Tibetan girls wear their hair so short? I've never seen any Tibetan girls with such short hair. *She laughs.*

After a while Tharlo says again: Your hair is too short.

The girl laughs again. I cut my hair short because I'm waiting for boys with long hair like you to come find me.

Tharlo is shocked by such a bold and suggestive remark. He doesn't know what to say. He moves his eyes away from the girl's face and starts looking around.

When she finishes drying his hair, she puts her hand on his shoulder. Her breasts

Tharlo: I don't know.

Shorthaired girl: [laughing] Don't you know who gave you your name?

[Tharlo stares at her in the mirror again.]

Shorthaired girl: [smiling] Why are you looking at me like that? Do I look that good?

Tharlo: I thought you were a man when I came in. Then I saw your earrings and necklace.

Shorthaired girl: Short hair is trendy in the city. This is in fashion.

Tharlo: Tibetan girls shouldn't wear their hair short. I've never seen any Tibetan girls with such short hair.

Shorthaired girl: [laughing, then a pause before speaking again] I cut my hair short because I'm waiting for boys with long hair like you to come find me.

[Tharlo is shocked by such a bold and suggestive remark. He doesn't know what to say. He moves his eyes away from the girl's face.]

Shorthaired girl: [looking at him in the mirror again, and with a touch of easiness in her voice] Look, with a bit of care you could be really cute.

Tharlo: [embarrassed, quickly taking out a fifty-yuan note from his satchel, and handing it to her] Here.

Shorthaired girl: [taking the note as Tharlo gets up from the chair] Don't you have anything smaller? I don't have change.

Tharlo: Don't worry, just keep it.

[Tharlo walks through the door, and is no longer seen in the frame. The shorthaired girl picks up his satchel and hat from the sofa and hands it to him near the door.]

Shorthaired girl: Don't you want your satchel? And your hat?

Tharlo's voice: Your towel.

[The shorthaired girl catches the towel Tharlo throws back to her, and watches him go off.]

are pressing on the back of Tharlo's head. She looks at him in the mirror again. There is a touch of easiness in her voice as she says to him: Look, with a bit of care you could be really cute.

Tharlo is embarrassed. He quickly takes out a fifty-yuan note from his satchel and hands it to her. Here.

She takes the note. Don't you have anything smaller? I don't have change.

Tharlo: Don't worry, just keep it. *Before she can say anything, he picks up the satchel with the lamb from the floor and dashes from the shop.*

Scene 8   Dekyi Photo Studio. Interior. Day.

Tharlo opens the door and looks inside. He enters the studio, and sees a few men there waiting.

Scene 6 **Dekyi Photo Studio. Interior. Day.**

Shot 11 *Medium shot. Filmed as mirror reflection. A few men are sitting by the wall waiting. Tharlo enters frame at lower left hand corner.*

Dekyi's voice: One, two, three.

[Camera clicks, and lights flash.]

Tharlo: *[to the men]* Are you here to take photos?

Men: Yes.

Tharlo: *[looking ahead to address Dekyi who is out of frame]* My hair is washed. Do I take the photo now?

Dekyi's voice: Wait a minute. I'll take yours soon.

Tharlo: Alright. I'll wait outside.

Dekyi: Alright.

[He goes out.]

Scene 9   Outside Dekyi Photo Studio. Exterior. Day.

Tharlo goes outside the studio into the street. He rolls a cigarette and smokes and looks towards the barbershop across the road. He sees the shorthaired girl standing outside the glass door, also looking at him. He continues to smoke and looks at her. She looks back and smiles.

Tharlo's little lamb bleats. He pulls the satchel to his front. The lamb pops his head out, looks at Tharlo and bleats again. Tharlo talks as if to himself: You are hungry again. Let me feed you. *Tharlo takes the milk bottle out from the satchel, and puts the teat in the lamb's mouth. The lamb sucks hard. Tharlo strokes the lamb's head and smiles. Then he looks across at the girl.*

Passers-by in the street look at Tharlo curiously. A few children come over and stroke the lamb on the head.

A customer arrives in the barbershop. The shorthaired girl enters with him.

Tharlo has almost finished the cigarette when a policeman walks by. He stares at Tharlo. Tharlo looks at the policeman, and grows nervous. He quickly throws away the butt. The policeman looks at the lamb. Where have you got this lamb from?

Tharlo is nervous. He's mine.

Policeman: What do you do?

Tharlo: I herd sheep.

Policeman: Did you steal this lamb?

Tharlo grows even more nervous. Did I steal it? Why should I steal my own lamb?

Policeman: Then why are you carrying it with you?

Tharlo: His mother was killed by a wolf. The other ewes won't take care of him. So I have to.

Policeman: Then why are you so nervous?

Tharlo: I'm not nervous.

Scene 7   **Outside Dekyi Photo Studio. Exterior. Day.**

Shot 12   *Wide shot. Filmed as reflection in a mirror inside the barbershop on the other side of the street. The mirror faces a glass window that looks into the street outside and the shops on the opposite side of the street, including Dekyi's photo studio. On the periphery of the frame are some fairy lights flashing around the window frame of the barbershop.*

[Tharlo is seen coming out of the studio, looking around, and sitting on his motorbike that is parked by the roadside. Then he rolls a cigarette, smokes, and looks towards the barbershop across the street. Although the sound of the traffic in the street is occasionally heard, the faint music from the radio is more consistent throughout this scene. The few words in the Chinese lyrics '…be a good person…' can be recognised in the refrain of the song.

The shorthaired girl walks towards the glass window into the periphery of the frame on the right. Her position is outside the camera focus area. She is eating some melon seeds as she looks outside at Tharlo. She has her back to the mirror, so her face is not seen in the reflection. On the left at the periphery of the frame, also outside the camera focus area, is some decorative fairy-lighting twinkling in the barbershop window.

She and Tharlo look at each other from across the street through the glass window. Tharlo notices his lamb stirring. He moves his eyes away from the shorthaired girl and feeds the lamb. Then he looks back at her.

A customer walks into the barbershop. The shorthaired girl goes in with him. They exit the frame. Tharlo's eyes follow them. Then a policeman enters the frame from the right, and walks towards Tharlo. The two are seen talking to each other.]

Policeman: But you look very nervous.

Tharlo looks at the policeman. I've always been afraid of policemen since I was little. I get scared as soon as I see one.

The policeman looks at the lamb, then tells Tharlo: Let me see your identity card.

Tharlo: I don't have one. I'm here to have a photo taken, so that I can have an identity card. You can ask the people in the photo studio if you don't believe me. *He points at the photo studio in front of them.*

The policeman looks at the studio. A few people come out. The policeman pushes Tharlo into the studio.

Scene 10   Dekyi Photo Studio. Interior. Day.

The policeman asks Dekyi as soon as they enter: This chap was sneaking around outside. He said he'd come to get a photo taken for his identity card. Is that true?

Dekyi: Yes, that's true. He's come to have a photo taken for his identity card. Chief Dorje sent him. I told him to go across the street to get his hair washed. He's ready for the photo now.

The policeman looks at Tharlo. He hasn't got an identity card. And the way he looked. I thought he was a thief.

Dekyi: No, no, he isn't.

Tharlo still looks nervous. The policeman looks at him. You haven't done any bad things. You don't have to be scared.

Tharlo: Well... well...

Dekyi: Look. You look different with just a little bit of cleaning up. You are rather handsome. *Then she looks at the policeman.* Isn't he just?

The policeman looks at Tharlo. Not bad-looking at all. He had that dishonest look back there outside.

Dekyi laughs. The policeman strokes the lamb on the head, and says to Dekyi: I'm getting going. See you. *Then he leaves.*

Tharlo waits until the policeman is definitely gone before he puts his satchel on a chair on one side. Then he goes and sits on a stool in front of the white backdrop. He watches the policeman leave the studio.

Dekyi picks up the camera and aims it at Tharlo. Good. Pay attention. Be more natural, more natural.

Tharlo gives a faint smile. Should I smile?

Dekyi: No, not really. Be serious. More serious. *Tharlo is slightly embarrassed as he adjusts his expression.*

Dekyi: Take off your amulet. You can't wear an amulet on your identity card. *Tharlo takes off his amulet, reluctantly.*

Scene 8   Dekyi Photo Studio. Interior. Day.

Shot 13   *Medium shot. Filmed as mirror reflection. The same area inside Dekyi's photo studio as Shot 11. The policeman enters the frame, and Tharlo follows.*

Policeman: *[as he enters]* This chap was sneaking around outside. He said he'd come to get a photo taken for his identity card. Is that true?

Dekyi's voice: Yes, that's true. He's come to have a photo taken for his identity card. Chief Dorje sent him. I told him to go across the street to get his hair washed. He's ready for the photo now. *[to Tharlo]* Take off your hat. Let's have a look. *[Tharlo takes off his hat.]*

Dekyi's voice: That's good. We can take your photo now.

Policeman: He was loitering outside with a lamb, and couldn't show his identity card. I thought he was a thief.

Dekyi's voice: No, no, he isn't.

[Tharlo still looks nervous.]

Policeman: *[looking at Tharlo]* You haven't done any bad things. You don't have to be scared.

Tharlo: I'm not scared.

Policeman: *[to Dekyi]* I'll get going. See you. *[exits]*

[Tharlo watches him leave.]

Dekyi's voice: Go and sit there. Let's take your photo now.

Tharlo: Alright.

Shot 14   *Medium close-up. Tharlo enters the frame and sits down in front of a white backdrop to form the same portrait dimension of a passport photo.*

Dekyi's voice: Good. Pay attention. Be more natural, more natural.

Dekyi's voice: Take off your hat. *[Tharlo takes his hat off.]*

Dekyi: Pay attention. Ready. Sit up. *Tharlo sits up. Dekyi presses the shutter, and says:* Done.

Tharlo: So quick?

Dekyi: Yes. *Tharlo sits there, almost not believing it is over.*

Dekyi walks over to the counter, and says to Tharlo who is still sitting in the chair: Over here, you pay now. Twenty yuan.

Tharlo goes over and pays. He takes out a fifty-yuan note and gives it to her.

Dekyi takes a look at the banknote and says: I'll get you the change. *Then she rummages through the drawer for the change.*

She asks Tharlo: Do you want to keep a copy of the photo for yourself?

Tharlo doesn't understand the question. What do you mean?

Dekyi: We don't need to print the photo. It's stored on a CD. You can have a few copies printed if you want.

Tharlo thinks for a moment. The photo is taken anyway. I might as well get a copy as a momento. I seldom get photos taken of me.

Dekyi: And you need an express. That's ten yuan more. Thirty altogether.

Tharlo: Alright.

Dekyi hands the change to Tharlo. Come back in half an hour for the photo. Don't forget your number: eighteen.

Tharlo: Don't I use my own name?

Dekyi: That's not necessary. Just say your number when you come back.

Tharlo: Fine. *He gets up and puts the satchel on his shoulder. Then he leaves.*

Dekyi's voice: Your satchel. *[Tharlo puts down his satchel.]*

Dekyi's voice: Take off your jacket as well. *[Tharlo takes his jacket off.]*

Dekyi's voice: Look here.

Tharlo: *[with a faint smile]* Should I smile?

Dekyi's voice: No, not really. Be serious. More serious. *[Tharlo is slightly embarrassed as he adjusts his expression.]*

Dekyi's voice: Take off your amulet.

Tharlo: This too?

Dekyi's voice: You can't wear any earrings, necklaces, or amulets in your identity card photo. *[Tharlo takes off his amulet, reluctantly.]*

Dekyi's voice: Pay attention. Ready. Sit up. *[Tharlo sits up.]*

Dekyi's voice: Look here. Place your ponytail behind. *[Tharlo places his ponytail behind.]*

Dekyi's voice: Tidy up your hair. *[Tharlo uses his palm to smooth his hair.]*

Dekyi's voice: Chest out. *[Tharlo straightens up.]*

Dekyi's voice: Left shoulder higher. *[Tharlo raises his left shoulder a little.]*

Dekyi's voice: Mouth slightly open. *[Tharlo opens his mouth slightly.]*

Dekyi's voice: Ready. One, two, three.

[Camera clicks and lights flash.]

Dekyi's voice: Done.

Tharlo: So quick?

Dekyi's voice: Yes.

[Tharlo puts on his hat, picks up his satchel, and exits the frame.]

Scene 11   The street outside Dekyi Photo Studio. Exterior. Day.

Tharlo stands by the roadside outside Dekyi Photo Studio looking around. The shorthaired girl looks around, lowers the curtain, and crosses the road to join him. Tharlo is nervous to see her coming towards him. He turns around to look at the studio. The girl stands next to him, and says, Tharlo! What are you doing here?

He looks at her, and says after a pause: I'm not doing anything, just standing.

Shorthaired girl: Have you got your photo done?

Tharlo: Yes. I can pick it up in half an hour. *She looks towards the studio.*

After a pause, Tharlo says: Just now you called my name like that. It felt strange.

Shorthaired girl: But why?

Tharlo: Because basically no one calls me by that name.

Shorthaired girl: I like your name. I don't want to call you Ponytail.

Tharlo doesn't say anything. He just looks at her. Then she continues: I saw you across the street. You really are very cute.

Tharlo: Am I? No one has ever said I am.

Shorthaired girl: I'm telling you the truth. Why should I lie to you?

Tharlo grows nervous again. She looks at him. He still looks at her, nervously. She laughs. Let's go to a karaoke bar tonight and have some fun.

Tharlo: I've never been. What's that?

Shorthaired girl: It's fun. A place people go to sing. You can sing any song you want to.

Tharlo: I can't sing.

She smiles. People who can't sing go to karaoke. You go and sing there. Then you can sing.

Tharlo becomes serious. I really can't sing.

Scene 9   **The street outside Dekyi Photo Studio. Exterior. Day.**

Shot 15   *Wide shot. Filmed as the reflection of a mirror in the barbershop opposite.*

[Tharlo is seen at the door of the photo studio. Various ambient sounds are heard. He looks around, crosses the road, and stands in front of the barbershop. The shorthaired girl goes outside her shop to join him. Now they are both in the foreground. The wide shot of Tharlo segues into a medium shot of them together.

Tharlo is nervous to see the shorthaired girl coming towards him. He turns around to look at the studio. The shorthaired girl stands next to him.]

Shorthaired girl: Hello, Tharlo! What are you doing here?

Tharlo: I'm not doing anything, just standing.

Shorthaired girl: Wait.

[The shorthaired girl exits, then enters frame again quickly with two ice-creams. She gives one to Tharlo.]

Shorthaired girl: Have an ice-cream. *[Tharlo takes the ice-cream from her.]* Have you got your photo done?

Tharlo: Yes. I can pick it up in half an hour.

[A pause.]

Tharlo: Just now you called my name like that. It felt strange.

Shorthaired girl: But why?

Tharlo: Because basically no one calls me by that name.

Shorthaired girl: I like your name. I don't want to call you Ponytail.

[Tharlo doesn't say anything. A pause.]

Shorthaired girl: I saw you across the street. You really are very cute.

Tharlo: No one has ever said I am.

Shorthaired girl: I'm telling you the truth. Why should I lie to you?

She looks at him. We'll go there, and I'll teach you.

Tharlo becomes nervous again. He looks at the people and the vehicles passing by. The traffic is busy. Noises of all kinds fill the street.

Scene 12   Dekyi Photo Studio. Interior. Day.

Close-up on Tharlo's passport photo. Tharlo picks up his photo and looks at it. He is standing in front of Dekyi.

Dekyi: Do you like it?

Tharlo: I look terrible!

Dekyi smiles. This is a passport photo, not a work of art.

Tharlo: But it really is bad.

Dekyi points at a passport photo in the display cabinet. Look. All passport photos look like this.

Tharlo says no more. Dekyi puts the photo in a paper bag, and gives it to Tharlo. Then she gives him a CD with Tharlo's name written on it. Give this to Chief Dorje.

Tharlo looks at Dekyi. Doubt is written all over his face. Dekyi says: Your passport photo is in there.

Tharlo still doesn't understand. He responds with a brief 'ah', then carefully puts the photo and the CD in his pocket.

Scene 13   Street. Exterior. Night.

Tharlo is riding his motorbike in the street with the girl on the pillion. A police car passes them by, sounding its siren and flashing its light.

[Tharlo grows nervous again and looks away. She looks at him. Another pause.]

Shorthaired girl: Let's go to a karaoke bar tonight and have some fun.

Tharlo: I've never been. What's that?

Shorthaired girl: It's fun. A place people go to sing. You can sing any song you want to.

Tharlo: I can't sing.

Shorthaired girl: *[smiles]* People who can't sing go to karaoke. You go and sing there. Then you can sing.

Tharlo: *[becoming serious]* I really can't sing.

Shorthaired girl: *[looking at him]* We'll go there, and I'll teach you.

[Tharlo smiles.]

Scene 10   A street. Exterior. Night.

Shot 16   Wide shot. Tharlo with the shorthaired girl on the pillion of his motorbike is driving from background to foreground of the frame.

[A police car passes them by, sounding its siren and flashing its light. The sound of the traffic gradually fades out as the girl's singing in the following scene fades in as voice-over to link the two scenes.]

Voice of Shorthaired girl: *[sings]* It is my destiny to meet you. / This is the song I sing for you…

Scene 14   Karaoke bar. Interior. Night.

The lights are dim in a room in the karaoke bar. Tharlo and the shorthaired girl sit on the sofa by the wall. Some cans of beer and snacks are scattered over the coffee table in front of them. They are drinking beer and eating. She holds a microphone in her hand and is about to sing.

The shorthaired girl calls towards the door: Excuse me! Excuse me! *A waiter comes through the door.*

Shorthaired girl: I want to sing 'It is My Destiny to Meet You'.

The waiter goes out with a brief 'yes'. The MV of 'It is My Destiny to Meet You' shows up on the TV screen. She looks at Tharlo, with the microphone in her hand, stands up and says to Tharlo: I'm singing. *Tharlo laughs happily.*

She starts singing. The song she sings is the Chinese version of 'It is My Destiny to Meet You'. From time to time her singing goes off key: My dearest, my sweetest, my most beloved, / My love for you / Is like the thistles in the mountain. / The thistles in the mountain.

She continues: Winding round the mountain / Is my love song like the river. / Bathing in that river is my heart. / Winding under the blue sky, my thoughts are like the road. / I travel with all my dreams in my knapsack. / All that waiting is nothing. / You are the choice of my life.

As she finishes the song, she picks up a beer and clinks it against Tharlo's bottle. She asks Tharlo: Do you like my singing?

Tharlo: You sing well.

Shorthaired girl: Do you understand what the song says.

Tharlo: I think I do.

She takes out a pack of cigarettes from her bag, pulls one out, lights it and starts smoking.

Tharlo looks at her. And you smoke.

She waves the cigarette in her hand lightly. It's for girls. They don't do much harm.

Tharlo: This is the first time I see a Tibetan girl smoke.

Scene 11   A room in a karaoke bar. Interior. Night.

*Shot 17   Full shot. The lights are dim in the room. The shorthaired girl is
singing to the TV in the foreground on the left. Tharlo is sitting
on a sofa further toward the back on the right-hand side.*

*[Beers and snacks are scattered over the coffee table. The song she sings is the
Chinese version of 'It is My Destiny to Meet You'. From time to time her
singing goes off key.]*

Shorthaired girl: *[sings]* My dearest, my sweetest, my most beloved, / My
love for you / Is like the thistles in the mountain. / The thistles in
the mountain.

*[As she pauses between the verses, she takes off her jacket, and throws it to
Tharlo. It lands on his head. He takes it off, and places it where she sat on
the sofa.]*

Shorthaired girl: *[continuing to sing]* Winding round the mountain / Is
my love song like the river. / Bathing in that river is my heart. / Winding
under the blue sky, my thoughts are like the road. / I travel with all my
dreams in my knapsack.

Shot 18   Medium shot. Tharlo sits on the right-hand seat of the sofa.

*[Suddenly one of the balloons on the back of the sofa bursts. The remnants fall on
the seat. Tharlo is slightly startled. He picks up the balloons and put them back
on the back of the sofa.]*

Shorthaired girl's voice: *[sings]* All that waiting is nothing. / You are the
choice of my life.

*[The shorthaired girl finishes the song, and walks into the frame to sit next to
Tharlo on the sofa.]*

Shorthaired girl: Do you like my singing?

Tharlo: You sing well.

Shorthaired girl: Do you understand what the song says.

Tharlo: I think I do.

Shorthaired girl: Many Tibetan girls smoke now. Just that you haven't seen any before. *Tharlo looks at the way she smokes. He can't get his head around it. She pulls another cigarette out from the pack.* Do you want to try one?

Tharlo: No.

Shorthaired girl: Don't you ever smoke?

Tharlo: I smoke. I roll my own.

The girl takes a puff of the cigarette, and blows out smoke in a circle. I see. To save money.

Tharlo looks at her. Not exactly.

She takes another puff. He looks at her. She puts out the cigarette. You look at me like I've murdered someone. It's fine. I won't smoke. *Tharlo smiles.*

Suddenly he remembers something. Is it really fine to leave my lamb at your place? I'm a bit worried.

Shorthaired girl: He'll be fine. Don't worry.

Tharlo doesn't say anything. She picks up a beer and clinks it against Tharlo's bottle again. Now, it's your turn. Sing me a song.

Tharlo: I really can't sing.

Shorthairl girl: I don't believe you.

Tharlo: I really can't sing. I swear I can't.

She thinks for a moment, then says: Why don't you sing me a la glu. I'm sure you know some la glu. All shepherds know them.

Tharlo: I don't know any.

Shorthaired girl: I don't believe you. *She laughs.* Stop pretending!

Tharlo is embarrassed. I only know one.

She is still laughing. Then sing me the one you know.

Tharlo: I don't sing well.

[*They drink. Then she moves towards him, takes his hat off, and touches his ponytail.*]

Shorthaired girl: You have a lovely ponytail.

[*Tharlo doesn't feel entirely comfortable with her teasing. She takes out a pack of cigarettes from her bag, pulls one out, lights it and starts smoking.*]

Tharlo: [*looking at her*] So you smoke.

Shorthaired girl: They're for girls. They don't do much harm.

Tharlo: It isn't right for Tibetan girls to smoke. This is the first time I've seen a Tibetan girl smoke.

Shorthaired girl: Many Tibetan girls smoke now. Just that you haven't seen any before.

Tharlo: [*looking at the way she smokes, and not able to get his head around it*] It isn't right.

Shorthaired girl: [*laughing, and pulling another cigarette out from the pack*] Do you want to try one?

Tharlo: No.

Girl: Don't you ever smoke?

Tharlo: I smoke. I roll my own.

Shorthaired girl: [*taking a puff of the cigarette, and blowing out smoke in a circle*] I see. To save money.

Tharlo: [*looking at her*] Not exactly.

[*She takes another puff.*]

Tharlo: [*looking at her*] It isn't right for Tibetan girls to smoke.

Shorthaired girl: [*laughing, and putting out the cigarette*] It's fine. I won't smoke. You look at me like I've murdered someone.

[*Tharlo smiles.*]

Shorthaired girl: Just sing!

Tharlo: I can't sing here. On the grassland I sometimes can sing a line or two.

Shorthaired girl: Come on, just sing! We've come to have fun. Drop your pretence.

Tharlo: I'm not pretending anything.

Shorthaired girl: Then sing.

Tharlo mutters his courage. Then I'll sing.

Shorthaired girl: Go on. *She hands the microphone to him.*

Tharlo avoids the microphone as if he's afraid of it. I don't use that thing. I don't use it.

She laughs. You'll sound good with it.

Tharlo: I'm not using it. I'll just sing without it.

She looks at him, and keeps forcing the microphone into his hand. Use it. Here everyone sings with it.

At last Tharlo takes it from her hand. He clears his throat, puts his hand on one cheek, and sings.

Tharlo sings: Let me sing a love song! / Fair maiden! / Flying in a familiar forest / Are two larks who did not know each other. / They were strangers once / But they have got to know each other as they listen to each other chirrup.

Tharlo doesn't sing well. His voice comes across as a shriek through the sound system. But he swells his song with true and rich feelings. He stops, and looks at the shorthaired girl. With embarrassment he says: I don't sing well.

Shorthaired girl: You sing very well. Go on. Isn't there another verse?

He puts the microphone back into the girl's hand. I won't sing with it. I'm not used to it.

The shorthaired girl gives up. Alright, alright. Just sing.

Tharlo: [suddenly remembering something] Is it really fine to leave my lamb in the barbershop?

Shorthaired girl: He'll be fine. Don't worry. [Tharlo doesn't say anything. She hands the microphone to him.] Now, it's your turn. Sing me a song.

Tharlo: I really can't sing.

Shorthaired girl: I don't believe you.

Tharlo: It's true.

Shorthaired girl: Why don't you sing me a la glu. I'm sure you know some la glu. All shepherds know them.

Tharlo: I don't know any.

Shorthaired girl: I don't believe you.

Tharlo: [embarrassed] I only know one.

Shorthaired girl: Then sing me the one you know.

Tharlo: I don't sing well.

Shorthaired girl: Stop pretending. Just sing!

Tharlo: This place makes me nervous. On the grassland I sometimes can sing a line or two.

Shorthaired girl: We've come to have fun. Just sing!

Tharlo: [taking off his jacket] Then I'll sing.

Tharlo: [avoiding the microphone she hands to him as if he is afraid of it] I don't use that thing. I don't use it.

Shorthaired girl: You'll sound good with it.

Tharlo: I'm not using it. I'll just sing without it.

Shorthaired girl: [looking at him, and forcing the microphone into his hand] Use it. Here everyone sings with it.

[At last Tharlo takes it from her hand. He stands up, walks to the other side of

Tharlo sings without the microphone: Let me sing a love song! / Fair maiden! / In a familiar village / Live those who are strangers to one other. / Who are destined to meet? / A few simple words will bring us together.

Tharlo stops singing. He feels slightly more natural now, but not altogether at ease. He is still nervous. He looks at the girl. Can you give me one of your cigarettes.

Shorthaired girl: I thought you liked your own roll-ups?

Tharlo: Mine are strong. I don't want to irritate you.

Shorthaired girl: It's fine. Smoke yours.

Tharlo: I won't smoke then.

Shorthaired girl: Then try one of mine.

Tharlo: Sure.

The girl smiles and gives him one, then lights it for him with a lighter.

Tharlo takes a heavy puff and spits it out. This tastes strange.

Shorthaired girl: It's menthol. It refreshes the mind.

Tharlo: Alright.

She looks at him. I bet you've sung this la glu to other girls, too.

Tharlo grows nervous. No, never. I've never sung to anyone before.

Shorthaired girl: Don't be nervous. I believe you.

Tharlo still wants to explain. I have never sung it to other girls.

Shorthaired girl: Can't you sing any other la glu?

Tharlo: I really can't.

She says casually: I wish you could sing a few more. They're nice.

Tharlo: When I go back, I'll learn a few more. Next time I'll sing them for you.

the room outside the frame. He starts singing. The first notes he sings are heard as voice-over.]

Shot 19   *Medium shot. Tharlo stands on the left hand side. To the right in the foreground is a TV screen playing the MV of another song.*

Tharlo: *[sings]* Let me sing a love song! / Fair maiden! / Flying in a familiar forest / Were two larks who did not know each other. / They were strangers once / But they have got to know each other as they listen to each other chirrup.

[Tharlo doesn't sing well. His voice comes across as a shriek through the sound system. But he swells his song with true and rich feelings. He stops, and looks at the shorthaired girl.]

Shorthaired girl's voice: You sing very well. Go on.

Tharlo: I told you I couldn't sing, and you made me.

Shorthaired girl's voice: Isn't there another verse? Go on.

Tharlo: *[putting the microphone down]* I won't sing with it. I'm not used to it.

Shorthaired girl's voice: Why do you stand with your back to me? Turn this way.

[Tharlo turns to face her.]

Tharlo: *[singing without the microphone]* Let me sing a love song! / Fair maiden! / In a familiar village / Live those who are strangers to each other. / Who are destined to meet? / A few words will bring us together. *[He finishes the verse, and goes towards her.]*

Shot 20   *Medium shot. Shorthaired girl is sitting on the left on the sofa, and Tharlo sits down on the right.*

Tharlo: *[feeling more natural now, and drinking some beer]* Can you give me one of your cigarettes?

Shorthaired girl: I thought you liked your own roll-ups?

Tharlo: Mine are strong. I don't want to irritate you.

After a while Tharlo looks at the girl, and asks her: Do you know any la glu?

The girl thinks for a moment. Actually I do a bit. I learnt a few when I tended sheep as a child.

Tharlo: Why don't you sing them now?

Shorthaired girl: I've forgotten them all. I can't remember any.

Tharlo: Just sing one.

She gives it some thought, and says: I really can't remember any. Let me sing you a pop song.

Tharlo takes another puff of the cigarette, and says: Alright.

The shorthaired girl calls towards the door. Excuse me! Can you just play any one pop song for me? *Music comes through the TV. She sings.*

Tharlo finishes one cigarette, and takes another one from the packet. He keeps smoking as he listens to her sing. Suddenly he is overcome by a violent cough. The shorthaired girl stops and asks, very concerned: Are you alright?

Tharlo: I get my cough attack. It happens sometimes when I smoke. *His cough grows more violent.*

She is very concerned. What should we do now? Should we go to the hospital?

Tharlo's cough is so violent that his face turns red. She hands him a beer. He pushes it away. I need rice wine. Only that works.

The shorthaired girl calls: Excuse me! Excuse me! Waiter! *A waiter comes in. She says to him:* Do you have rice wine?

Waiter: No, we don't.

The shorthaired girl takes out a fifty-yuan note. Go and buy a bottle of rice wine for me. Any kind.

Waiter: We don't allow consumption of rice wine here.

Tharlo's head hits the coffee table. A few beer bottles fall off. The waiter is shocked. He looks at Tharlo.

Shorthaired girl: It's fine. Smoke yours.

Tharlo: I won't smoke then.

Shorthaired girl: Then try one of mine. *[She smiles and gives him one, then lights it for him with a lighter.]*

Tharlo: *[taking a few puffs]* This tastes strange.

Shorthaired girl: It's different. It feels cool in the mouth.

Tharlo: *[putting out the cigarette]* I don't like this.

[They drink.]

Tharlo: I'm not used to sitting like this. *[He puts his feet on the sofa and sits with his legs crossed.]*

Shorthaired girl: *[laughing]* You can't put your feet on that.

[Tharlo responds with a quiet 'damn!', then puts his feet down.]

Shorthaired girl: *[looking at him]* I bet you've sung this la glu to other girls, too.

Tharlo: *[growing nervous]* No, never.

Shorthaired girl: Don't be nervous. I believe you.

Tharlo: *[still wanting to explain]* I have never sung it to other girls.

Shorthaired girl: *[casually]* I wish you could sing a few more. They're nice.

Tharlo: When I go back, I'll learn a few more. Next time I'll sing them for you. *[pause]* Do you know any la glu?

Shorthaired girl: *[thinking for a moment]* Actually I do a bit. I learnt a few when I tended sheep as a child.

Tharlo: Why don't you sing one now?

Shorthaired girl: I've forgotten them all. I can't remember any.

Tharlo: Just sing one.

Shorthaired girl: He sometimes has this cough. When it happens, only rice wine can stop it.

The waiter goes out with the money, not totally convinced. The TV is playing a karaoke song. The MV shows some men and women flirting. Soon the waiter comes back with a bottle of rice wine. He gives the shorthaired girl her change. She tips him with a ten-yuan note.

Tharlo has already taken off the lid of the bottle. She picks up a beer. Drink up, I'll drink with you. *They start drinking. She takes a sip, and stops to look at him.*

Tharlo doesn't seem to want to stop, and pours the rice wine down his throat. He only stops after he has emptied half the bottle. Then he heaves a long sigh, and ceases coughing.

Shorthaired girl: *[giving it some thought]* I really can't remember any. Let me sing you a pop song.

Tharlo: *[taking another puff of the cigarette]* Alright.

Shorthaired girl: *[calling towards the door]* Excuse me!

Waiter 's voice: Yes!

Shorthaired girl: Do you have 'I Want to Leave the Mountains'?

Waiter 's voice: Yes.

Shorthaired girl: I'll sing that one.

[Music starts. She gets up from the sofa and goes toward the TV. She exits the frame.]

Shorthaired girl's voice: *[sings]* La...la...la... / I want to leave the mountains. / I want to see the world outside. / I want to leave the mountains. / I want to see the world outside...

[Tharlo finishes one cigarette, and takes another from the packet. He keeps smoking as he listens to her sing. Suddenly he is overcome by a violent cough. The shorthaired girl stops singing. She comes back inside the frame and sits next to him.]

Shorthaired girl: Are you alright?

Tharlo: I get my cough attack. It happens sometimes when I smoke. *[His cough grows more violent.]*

Shorthaired girl: *[looking concerned]* What should we do now? Should we go to the hospital?

[Tharlo's cough is very bad. She hands him a beer. He pushes it away.]

Tharlo: I need rice wine. Only that works.

Shorthaired girl: *[calling]* Excuse me! Excuse me! Waiter!

Waiter 's voice: Yes.

Shorthaired girl: Do you have rice wine?

Scene 15   Barbershop. Interior. Morning.

Sunbeams come through the curtains to light up the room. It lights up Tharlo's face and the face of the girl next to him. Tharlo wakes up, and finds himself lying under the blanket shirtless. The shorthaired girl is lying by his side. He has no idea where he is. He gets up, looks at her still sleeping by his side. Quietly he puts on his clothes, and walks across to sit in the barber's chair. He looks at himself in the mirror. He looks puzzled in the mirror as if he doesn't know what to do.

He hears the voice of the shorthaired girl behind him. You're up already.

Tharlo turns back to look at her nervously. Why am I here?

The shorthaired girl is still lying on the sofa bed. She smiles at him. Then she sits up. Last night your cough was very bad. So you drank a lot of rice wine. I couldn't stop you. Then you got drunk, and I brought you back here.

Waiter 's voice: No, we don't.

Shorthaired girl: *[taking out a fifty-yuan note]* Go and buy a bottle of rice wine for me. Any kind.

Waiter 's voice: We don't allow consumption of rice wine here.

Shorthaired girl: He sometimes has this cough. When it happens, only rice wine can stop it. *[She hands some money to the waiter who is outside the frame.]*

Shot 21   *Medium shot. Shot from behind Tharlo and the shorthaired girl and facing the door of the room.*

[The waiter opens the door, and comes in with a bottle of rice wine. He gives the shorthaired girl her change, looks at Tharlo, and goes out. She takes the lid off the rice wine, and hands it to Tharlo.]

Shorthaired girl: Drink up.

[Tharlo takes the bottle from her, and gulps it down. He only stops after he has emptied half the bottle. Then he heaves a long sigh, and ceases coughing.]

Scene 12   Barbershop. Interior. Morning.

Shot 22   *Full shot. Filmed as mirror reflection. Two pairs of bare feet are seen on the sofa emerging from under a blanket. After a while, one pair of feet stirs.*

[Tharlo awakes, and sits up. Now his whole person is inside the frame. He finds himself shirtless, with the shorthaired girl lying by his side. He has no idea where he is. Then he gets up, looks at her still sleeping, and quietly puts on his clothes. He walks over to sit in the barber's chair in front of the mirror. He looks puzzled in the mirror as if he doesn't know what to do. The shorthaired girl also awakes and sits up. She looks at him in the mirror.]

Shorthaired girl: *[from behind Tharlo]* You're up already.

Tharlo: Why am I here?

Shorthaired girl: Last night your cough was very bad. So you drank a lot

Tharlo: Was that so?

She keeps smiling at him. He dares not look at her. She says: Do you really like me?

Tharlo doesn't know what to say. What are you saying?

Shorthaired girl: Last night you said you liked me.

He still doesn't know what to say. Did I?

Shorthaired girl: Don't worry. I'm not going to hold you to anything.

Tharlo is very nervous. He sits in the chair motionless. She continues: It's true. Last night you said you liked me.

He looks at himself in the mirror, looking increasingly nervous. She gets up and puts a jacket round her own shoulders, then wets a towel and comes over to wipe Tharlo's face for him. She strokes Tharlo's ponytail: I like your ponytail.

Tharlo grows more nervous. She continues: You were very drunk last night. I almost had to carry you on my back. *Tharlo looks at her with very doubtful eyes.*

Shorthaired girl: It's true. I also pushed your motorbike back here. It's outside now. *Tharlo keeps looking at her. She puts her head on his shoulder.*

Shorthaired girl: Take me somewhere else. I don't want to stay here any longer.

At last Tharlo finds something to say: I've never been anywhere.

Shorthaired girl: Then I'll take you to places. We can go to Lhasa, Beijing, Shanghai, Guangzhou and Hong Kong. Anywhere we want.

Tharlo: I've never thought about going to those places.

Shorthaired girl: Where would you go if you were to choose?

Tharlo: Lhasa, of course.

Shorthaired girl: And then?

Tharlo thinks for a moment. Beijing Tian'anmen.

of rice wine. I couldn't stop you. Then you got drunk, and I brought you back here.

Tharlo: Was that so?

[She keeps looking at him in the mirror. He dares not look at her.]

Shorthaired girl: Do you really like me?

Tharlo: *[not knowing what to say]* What do you mean?

Shorthaired girl: Last night you said you liked me.

Tharlo: *[still not knowing what to say]* Did I?

Shorthaired girl: Don't worry. I'm not going to hold you to anything.

[Tharlo is very nervous. He sits in the chair motionless.]

Shorthaired girl: It's true. Last night you said you liked me.

[She gets up from the sofa, wets a towel, comes towards Tharlo, and hands it to him. Her torso is seen standing behind him, but her face is above the top edge of the frame. He takes the towel from her, and wipes his face.]

Shorthaired girl: *[stroking Tharlo's ponytail]* I like your ponytail. *[Tharlo grows more nervous.]* You were very drunk last night. I almost had to carry you on my back.

[Tharlo says nothing.]

Shorthaired girl: It's true. I also pushed your motorbike back here. It's outside now.

[She rests her elbows on his shoulder, and her hands on his chest. She dips her head, so that her face is close to his. Now her head is inside the frame but she faces downward, so her face is only partially visible.]

Shorthaired girl: Take me somewhere else. I don't want to stay here any longer.

Tharlo: *[at last finding something to say]* I've never been anywhere.

Shorthaired girl: Then I'll take you to places. Anywhere is good for us.

She laughs. And then?

Tharlo: New York of America.

Shorthaired girl: You know so many places.

Tharlo laughs. The girl laughs, too, and says: We won't make it to New York. That'd take a lot of money. Let's go to Lhasa. That we can do.

Tharlo: People say that takes a lot of money, too. I don't have enough money.

She says without a thought: Sell your sheep. Then we'll have money.

Tharlo: They aren't all mine. Some belong to other people.

Shorthaired girl: That's alright. As long as you want to go, we'll think of a way. I can make some money here at this barbershop. When we have enough money, you'll take me to Lhasa and Beijing.

Tharlo keeps looking at her. The lamb bleats. Tharlo looks in the direction of the sound. The lamb pops his head out from the satchel by the wall. She says: Don't worry. I fed him last night. *Tharlo looks at her, with trust in his eyes.*

After a while Tharlo says: I should go.

He packs his things. She watches him. He puts the satchel on his shoulder. She walks over to him, and kisses him on the cheek. He looks at himself in the mirror. Suddenly he freezes. After a while he opens the door and goes out. He shuts the door behind him.

She looks at the door, then goes to sit in the barber's chair, and turns her face to the mirror. She stares at herself in the mirror for a long time. There isn't much expression on her face.

After a while Tharlo opens the door from outside. He pops half of his head through the door and asks the girl: What is your name?

She turns to him with a smile: My name is Yangtso.

Tharlo's half head utters a half 'right', then retreats. He shuts the door behind him. The engine of a motorbike outside the barbershop is heard. Then the sound recedes into the distance. The shorthaired girl looks at herself in the mirror again. She looks thoughtful.

We can go to Lhasa, Beijing, Shanghai, Guangzhou and Hong Kong. Anywhere we want.

Tharlo: I've never thought about going to those places.

Shorthaired girl: Where would you go if you were to choose?

Tharlo: Lhasa, of course.

Shorthaired girl: And then?

Tharlo: [thinking for a moment] Beijing Tian'anmen.

Shorthaired girl: And then?

Tharlo: New York of America.

Shorthaired girl: [laughing] You know so many places.

[Tharlo laughs, too.]

Shorthaired girl: We won't make it to New York. That'd take a lot of money. Let's go to Lhasa. That we can do.

Tharlo: People say that takes a lot of money, too. I don't have enough money.

Shorthaired girl: [without a thought] Sell your sheep. Then we'll have money.

Tharlo: They aren't all mine. Some belong to other people.

Shorthaired girl: That's alright. As long as you want to go, we'll think of a way. I can make some money here at this barbershop. When we have enough money, I'll take you to Lhasa first, then Beijing.

[The lamb bleats. They look in the direction of the sound. The shorthaired girl straightens up. Her face is no longer in the frame.]

Shorthaired girl's voice: Don't worry. I fed him last night.

[Tharlo turns back to face the mirror. There is a look of trust and ease in his eyes.]

Tharlo: [suddenly remembering something] I must go.

[He gets up, and walks towards the door. Although both their faces are now

Scene 16   Street. Exterior. Day.

Tharlo is riding through a street in town on his motorbike. There is a cheerful atmosphere everywhere. He stops in front of a grocery store, parks his motorbike outside, and enters.

Scene 17   Grocery store. Interior. Day.

Tharlo walks directly to the counter, and looks around. The shopkeeper approaches him and asks him: Can I help you?

Tharlo: I need some firecrackers.

Shopkeeper: What kind of firecrackers do you want?

Tharlo: I want the double-blast type. Fifty of those.

Shopkeeper: So many?

Tharlo smiles. And ten boxes of matches.

The shopkeeper brings over two big boxes of double-blast firecrackers. Then she calculates the costs on a sounding calculator. One hundred and twenty.

Tharlo takes out one hundred and twenty yuan, and hands it to the shopkeeper.

Shopkeeper: Anything else?

Tharlo: A case of rice wine, please.

above the frame and no longer visible, it is clear from their movement that she leans over to him, and kisses him on the cheek. Then he picks up his things, goes towards the door, and exits the frame.]

Tharlo's voice: What is your name?

Shorthaired girl's voice: My name is Yangtso.

Scene 13   A street. Exterior. Day.

Shot 23   Wide shot. The depth of the shot extends from the shops in the foreground to the mountains far away in the background. Street noises and music coming from the radio are heard.

[Tharlo is riding in town on his motorbike. To his left is a long terrace of houses. He stops in front of a grocery store, and enters.]

Scene 14   Grocery store. Interior. Day.

Shot 24   Full shot. Filmed as the reflection of a mirror on the wall opposite to the counter.

[Tharlo enters the frame, then stands in front of the counter with his back to the mirror. The music coming from the radio is now louder.]

Shopkeeper: Can I help you?

Tharlo: I need some firecrackers.

Shopkeeper: What kind of firecrackers do you want?

Tharlo: I want the double-blast type. Fifty of those.

[The shopkeeper goes to the shelf on the right outside the frame, then comes back with the firecrackers.]

The shopkeeper looks at him, and asks: Which brand?

Tharlo: Something cheap. It's only for myself.

Shopkeeper: Alright. Anything else?

Tharlo: Nothing.

Scene 18   On the road back to the police station. Exterior. Day.

Tharlo is riding on the motorbike on the road. The pillion and bags on both sides are full of the items he has bought. He looks serious. He has a lot on his mind.

Scene 19   Township police station. Interior. Day.

Tharlo enters the police office, and stands there. His hair is glossy. His ponytail is also neatly tied up. He looks very decent. The police chief looks at him. One trip to town has made you so much more handsome!

Tharlo hesitates, but at last says to Chief Dorje: I might have met a bad person.

The police chief is alarmed. You have to report to us at once when you see bad people.

Tharlo: Now I can't be sure whether it really is a bad person.

Shopkeeper: Anything else?

Tharlo: And ten boxes of matches.

[*She brings over the matches. Then she calculates the costs on a sounding calculator.*]

Shopkeeper: One hundred and twenty.

[*He hands her some money, and she gives him back the change.*]

Tharlo: Do you have any cheap rice wine? It's for myself.

Shopkeeper: [*taking a bottle down the shelf behind her*] What about this one?

Tharlo: How much is it?

Shopkeeper: Five fifty.

Tharlo: I'll take one case.

Scene 15   **A road. Exterior. Day.**

Shot 25   *Wide shot. Tharlo is riding with his back to the camera towards the mountain range in the distance. There are expansive stretches of land on both sides of the road. On the right hand side of the road some barbed wire is glimpsed. The pillion and bags on both sides are full of the items he has bought.*

[*At the end of this scene Tharlo's voice is heard as voice-over addressing Chief Dorje.*]

Scene 16   **Township police station. Interior. Day.**

Shot 26   *Full shot. Tharlo and Chief Dorje sitting at opposite desks under the slogan 'Serve the People'. In the foreground is the iron stove with a kettle still steaming. The pipe of the stove extends upward to visually divide the space into two, with Tharlo and Chief Dorje on either side.*

The police chief smiles. Ponytail, you must have proof when you report a bad person. Otherwise, you will bear the full legal responsibility. *Tharlo seems as if he is choking on something. He falls silent.*

The police chief asks: Have you done the photo for your identity card?

Tharlo takes out the photo and the CD, and hands them to the police chief. I look terrible.

The police chief looks at the photo. This is a passport photo. It should look like this. *Tharlo says nothing more. The police chief puts away the CD, and registers receipt of it in a book.*

Tharlo looks at the photo Chief Dorje gives back to him. Don't you need this photo?

Police chief: No. Your photo is in the CD. *Tharlo responds with a quiet 'yes'. The police chief continues:* You have to pay an administrative cost of thirty yuan for the identity card. *Tharlo takes out thirty yuan, and gives it to him. The police chief finishes the registration, and gives him a receipt.* This is done now. Come back in a month to get your card.

Tharlo: Is the identity card really so important?

Police chief: Of course. With your identity card people will know who you are.

Tharlo: Even with it people in big places such as Lhasa or Beijing wouldn't know who I am.

The police chief smiles. We aren't talking about the same thing. You'll find out. Now, go.

Tharlo: But yesterday a policeman asked whether I had an identity card. It really seems to be a rather important thing.

Police chief: I'm glad you've realised how important it is.

Tharlo says nothing more, but he still looks puzzled.

The police chief suddenly thinks about something. Where did you stay last night without an identity card?

Tharlo: [hesitating, but at last to Chief Dorje] I might have met a bad person.

Police chief: [alarmed] You have to report to us at once when you see bad people.

Tharlo: Now I can't be sure whether it really is a bad person.

Police chief: If you see bad people, you have to report them, and you must have proof. Otherwise, you will bear the full legal responsibility.

[Tharlo falls silent.]

Police chief: Have you brought the photo for your identity card with you?

Tharlo: [taking out the photo and the CD, and handing them to the police chief] I look terrible.

Police chief: [looking at the photo] This is a passport photo. It's alright as long as people can recognise it's you. [He keeps the CD, returns the photo to Tharlo.] Your photo is in the CD. [Tharlo takes the photo from him.] Now you have to pay an administrative cost of thirty yuan for the identity card.

[The police chief walks away, then comes back with a receipt book. Meanwhile, Tharlo takes out thirty yuan, and puts it on the desk. The police chief starts to write a receipt for him. Suddenly, Tharlo's lamb bleats. He takes out its milk bottle.]

Tharlo: Chief Dorje.

Police chief: Yes?

Tharlo: My lamb is hungry. Can I get a little hot water for his milk?

Police chief: Of course. It's just boiled.

Tharlo: Thank you.

[Tharlo walks towards the iron stove in the foreground, and pours some hot water from the kettle into the milk bottle. Then he goes back to the chair, and feeds the lamb.]

Tharlo: Chief Dorje, aren't your colleagues back yet?

Police chief: [still writing the receipt] No. They're still out on a case. [He

Tharlo grows slightly nervous. I stayed with a friend.

Police chief: That was fortuitous. No inns would have taken you.

Tharlo is about to get up from his seat and leave when the police chief speaks again: Let me ask you a personal question: Why have you kept the ponytail?

Tharlo straightens his back and begins: This . . .

The police chief is interested. This what . . . ?

Tharlo looks at him. There's no reason, really.

The police chief is disappointed. It's fine if you don't want to tell me. It's your right not to.

Tharlo looks at him again. It's nothing important. It was just a film I saw.

The police chief becomes interested again. What do you mean?

Tharlo: When I graduated from primary school, before I went up to the mountains, I had some money from the people who had hired me to tend their sheep. I went into town.

Police chief: And then?

Tharlo: I watched a movie there.

Police chief: What did it have to do with your ponytail?

Tharlo: I grew it after watching the movie.

Police chief: What was the connection?

Tharlo: There was a man with a ponytail in the movie. Women liked him.

The police chief laughs out loud. Have you gotten women to like you since you've grown your ponytail?

Tharlo: Women in our village don't like me. They say I'm too poor.

The police chief stops laughing. What was the movie called?

finishes writing the receipt, and gives it to Tharlo.] Here you are. Come back in a month to get your card.

Tharlo: This isn't necessary.

Police chief: You must keep it, otherwise you won't get your card.

Tharlo: *[taking the receipt]* I'm afraid I might lose it. *[putting the receipt in his pocket]* Chief Dorje, is the identity card really so important?

Police chief: Of course. With your identity card people will know who you are.

Tharlo: Even with it people in Lhasa, or Beijing, or other places wouldn't know who I am.

Police chief: With an identity card people would know who you are. Otherwise, how would they know?

Tharlo: Yesterday a policeman asked whether I had an identity card. I said I didn't. He said I looked like a thief.

Police chief: That's why you need an identity card.

[Tharlo says nothing more, but he still looks puzzled.]

Police chief: *[suddenly thinking about something]* Where did you stay last night without an identity card?

Tharlo: *[growing slightly nervous]* I stayed with a friend.

Tharlo: I don't know. People said it was a foreign movie, so I went. Afterwards, I told many people about the story. No one said they'd seen it.

The police chief says with regret: I must find time to see that movie.

Scene 20 Mountain road. Exterior. Night.

Tharlo is riding along a mountain road on his motorbike. The headlight of the motorbike pierces the darkness of the night.

Scene 21 Tharlo's mountain shed. Interior. Night.

It is rather dark in the shed. A lamp is lit. The fire in the stove is burning. The cracking noise of twigs and branches burning is audible. Tharlo is sitting to the left of the stove. He has wrapped himself in a robe. He pours some tea into a bowl, then adds in yak butter, diary dregs, and barley flour. He slowly rubs them with his fingers to form barley cakes. Then he slowly pours some strong tea in the bowl, and starts eating. He eats very slowly, taking it mouthful by mouthful, and occasionally sipping tea. After he finishes the barley cake, he drinks more tea, equally slowly.

Wolf cries are heard from outside. The barking of his dog outside is also heard.

Tharlo seems to be very accustomed to these sounds. He does not appear to be disturbed by the sounds, and continues to drink tea. Then he takes some tobacco and a shred of newspaper to roll a cigarette. He lights it and smokes. When he finishes the cigarette, he takes another sip of the tea.

After a while he gets up, picks up a torch from the cutlery shelf on the wall, and switches it on. Then he looks for something else. He finds some double-blast firecrackers, and brings them out with him.

Scene 17   **Mountain road. Exterior. Night.**

Shot 27   *Extreme wide shot from high angle. Tharlo is riding along a mountain road on his motorbike, crossing the frame from left to right. The headlight of the motorbike pierces the darkness of night.*

Scene 18   **Tharlo's mountain shed. Interior. Night.**

Shot 28   *Medium shot. Tharlo from the sideview is sitting and smoking on the left hand side of the frame. A lamp is lit on the table on the right hand side in the foreground.*

[It is rather dark in the shed. Something on the stove is steaming. The cracking noise of twigs and branches burning is audible. Tharlo has wrapped himself in a robe. Wolf cries and the barking of dogs are heard from outside. Tharlo seems to be very accustomed to these sounds. After a while he switches on a torch, gets up, and takes out some firecrackers from a box.]

Scene 22   **Tharlo's shed in the mountain. Exterior. Night.**

Tharlo walks outside the shed with the torch. The bleating of sheep and a dog barking echo in the dark. He walks on. Distant wolf-howls are audible. He walks further on. After a few steps he stops, squats down, and tries to light something with matches. After a while the loud noise of a double-blast firecracker is heard. The air under the dark sky feels shaken. He lights two more double-blast firecrackers. Wolf howls stop. Sheep bleating also stops. Tharlo stands up, and cries into the distance. His voice echoes in the dark of the night. He pees.

Scene 23   **Tharlo's mountain shed. Interior. Night.**

Tharlo goes back inside his shed. He pokes the fire, and adds some sheep dung into it. Then he climbs into his platform-bed built with earth. He picks up an alarm-clock by the bedside, sets it at seven, winds it, and leaves it on the small bedside table. He blows out the lamp.

Scene 24   **Outside the sheep pen. Exterior. Night.**

The sky is thickly dotted with stars. Occasional sheep-bleating and dog-barking are heard.

Scene 19   **Outside Tharlo's mountain shed. Exterior. Night.**

Shot 29   *Extreme wide shot. The light spilling out from Tharlo's shed is enveloped by the vast darkness of the surroundings. The only other source of light is the moon in the sky that appears very small on the upper left of the frame. Tharlo walks outside the shed with the torch creating a third—and mobile—light source.*

[The bleating of sheep and the barking of a dog echo in the dark. He walks on. Wolf howls in the distance are audible. He walks further on. After a few steps he stops, squats down, and tries to light something with matches. After a while the loud noise of a double-blast firecracker is heard, and the burst of the explosion can be seen. The dark sky appears to be shaken by the blast. He lights two more double-blast firecrackers. Wolf howls cease. Sheep bleating also ceases. Tharlo stands up, and the sound of his cry resounds in the distance and is swallowed up in the dark of the night.]

Scene 20   **Outside the sheep pen. Exterior. Night.**

Shot 30   *Wide shot of the sky. A high voltage electricity pylon stands erect in the moonlight. Cables extend from the pylon into the distance.*

[Occasional sheep-bleating and dog-barking are heard, followed by a song coming from the radio.]

Scene 21   **Tharlo's mountain shed. Interior. Night.**

Shot 31   *Medium shot of Tharlo's feet. He is lying on his platform-bed built of earth. He is holding a transistor radio in his hand and is listening to la glu folk songs. The same song from the radio can be heard more clearly now.*

The song on the radio: Pilgrims of Ü-Tsang! / Have you come in faith and sincerity? / Without a sincere heart, / Don't meddle with Buddha, / Don't spend your day performing prostration. / My loved one afar! / Have you given your heart to me? / Without a true heart, / Don't meddle with me, / Don't spend your days delighting me with your laughs, / Don't make vows you cannot keep to cause misery…

Scene 25 Tharlo's mountain shed. Interior. Morning.

Close-up on an alarm clock. The clock hands are pointing to seven o'clock. The alarm rings to wake Tharlo up. He gets up, puts a robe around his shoulder, and goes out.

Scene 26 Outside the sheep pen. Exterior. Morning.

Tharlo's old dog sees him approach, and wags his tail. Tharlo walks towards the sheep pen, stands at the perimeter, and looks on. Some sheep bleat; some are prone on the ground ruminating. Occasional sound of bleating continues. Tharlo walks to the other side, still with the robe on his shoulders. He pees towards the distance. The sound of his pee hitting the ground is heard. When he finishes, he turns to go back inside the shed.

Scene 27 Tharlo's mountain shed. Interior. Morning.

Tharlo washes his face. The kettle is on the stove.

Scene 28 Outside the sheep pen. Exterior. Morning.

Tharlo brings his teapot outside. He pays respect to spirits in the four corners of the earth by spooning out tea with a metal ladle in four directions. As he does this, he murmurs prayers. He feeds the dog. Then he counts the sheep one by one carefully. He brings the sheep up the slope. He moves slowly so as not to hurry them. The sheep climb a hill on the opposite side, and eat grass on the way.

Scene 29 A road. Exterior. Day.

Tharlo is driving fast on a road meandering through the grassland. Two big rectangular plastic buckets are fixed on the pillion. On both sides of the bumper are a few other plastic bottles.

Scene 22   Tharlo's mountain shed. Interior. Morning.

Shot 32   *Medium shot. Tharlo's torso is seen in the bottom right-hand corner of the frame. He is washing his face. On the left-hand side of the frame is a kettle boiling on the stove.*

Scene 23   Outside the sheep pen. Exterior. Morning.

Shot 33   *Extreme wide shot. Tharlo's head is seen above a low mud wall. He is moving into the open area from the rough covered corridor outside his shed. His whole person comes into view, as he walks into the open area. Two scarecrows are visible nearby.*

[Tharlo has brought his teapot with him. He pays respect to the spirits in the four corners by spreading tea with a ladle in four directions. As he does so, he murmurs prayers.]

Shot 34   *Extreme wide shot. Tharlo stands on the edge of the sheep pen with his back to the camera watching the sheep return to the pen.*

Scene 30   By a stream. Exterior. Day.

Tharlo fills a bucket of water, and drinks it. He raises the bucket in such a way that it covers his entire face. The noise of him drinking is heard. When he finishes drinking, he looks content. He gets another bucket of water to fill the vessels he's brought with him. Then he carries the two filled vessels to the motorbike, and fixes them on the pillion with some ropes. He gets on the motorbike, starts the engine, and drives away.

Scene 31   A road. Exterior. Day.

Tharlo on his motorbike drives along the stream. He sees a dead donkey hanging on a cliff. It was probably killed when it fell off the cliff. He stops, and looks at the dead donkey. He becomes immersed in deep thought. After a while he starts the motorbike again and rides away.

Scene 32   A road. Exterior. Day.

Tharlo on his motorbike meanders along the mountain roads.

Scene 24   At a well. Exterior. Day.

Shot 35   *Wide shot. Tharlo has stopped his motorbike next to a well. In the background is a hill rising steeply behind him. A few plastic containers are attached to either side of his motorbike.*

[*Tharlo fills a container on his bike from a metal bucket. Then he fetches another bucket of water from the well.*]

Shot 36   *Medium shot.*

[*Tharlo drinks water from the metal bucket. He raises it in such a way that it covers his entire face. Drinking sounds can be heard.*]

Shot 37   *Close-up on the surface of the water in the well. A vague reflection of Tharlo in the water is seen. The reflection is unclear and unstable as the water is disturbed.*

Scene 25   A road. Exterior. Day.

Shot 38   *Extreme wide shot. Tharlo on his motorbike drives into the frame from the left and out to the right. The road runs parallel to the horizontal axis of the frame and the continuous ridges of the hills in the background. On top of the hills are two high-voltage pylons with electric cables running through them.*

Scene 26   Outside Tharlo's mountain shed. Exterior. Day.

Shot 39   *Extreme wide shot. Tharlo's motorbike is on the left. He walks to the right into his shed carrying two buckets of water. His route is parallel to the horizontal axis of the frame, and to the continuous ridges of the hills in the background.*

Scene 33   Tharlo's mountain shed. Interior. Day.

Tharlo pours water into a water tank.

Scene 34   Grassland. Exterior. Day.

Tharlo's sheep scatter in groups on the hill. He approaches them on his motorbike and watches them leisurely grazing. Another herd of sheep approaches. The two herds are about to mingle.

On the slope opposite tending the other herd is a girl who has the lower part of her face covered with a scarf. She stands up and calls to Tharlo: Ponytail, please drive my sheep this way.

Tharlo sits on his motorbike. He doesn't move. She raises her voice and shouts: Hey, do you hear me?

Tharlo sits up, starts the engine and drives toward her sheep. He honks, and drives in a circle around them. Her sheep go back in her direction. Tharlo switches off the engine, and remains sitting on his motorbike.

She sits down on the grass, and says 'thank you' to Tharlo.

Still sitting on his motorbike, Tharlo looks towards her and asks: Can I ask a favour from you?

Girl whose lower face is covered with a scarf: What is it?

Tharlo: Can you sing me a la glu?

She laughs. You aren't my sweetheart. Why should I sing you a la glu?

Tharlo: I have no other intentions. I just want to hear a la glu.

Scene 27   **Tharlo's mountain shed. Interior. Day.**

Shot 40   *Full shot. Tharlo is on the left hand side in the background, pouring water into the water-tank. On the left in the foreground is the lamp on the table, which is unlit. Light comes through the door on the right.*

Scene 28   **Outside the sheep pen. Exterior. Evening.**

Shot 41   *Extreme wide shot from high angle of Tharlo ushering the sheep back into the sheep pen.*

Girl whose lower face is covered with a scarf: You're my senior. I'm too shy to sing to you.

Tharlo doesn't say anything. She asks him: Why do you want to hear a la glu?

Tharlo: There isn't any reason.

Girl whose lower face is covered with a scarf: Then why do you want to hear it?

Tharlo thinks for a while. If you don't want to sing for me, what about teaching me to sing?

Girl whose lower face is covered with a scarf: Why do you want to learn the la glu?

Tharlo: There is no reason. I just want to learn a couple of la glu. *She laughs.*

Tharlo: Why do you laugh?

Girl whose lower face is covered with a scarf: Nothing, nothing, really.

Tharlo: Teach me. I'll pay you for teaching me.

She laughs. How much would you pay me?

Tharlo: Ten yuan for a la glu.

She laughs again. Alright. I'll teach you. I can teach you a hundred la glu every day.

Tharlo: I don't want to learn that many. Just teach me a few.

Girl whose lower face is covered with a scarf: Which type do you want to learn? There are many types of la glu. Some are sung when the couple first meet. Some are sung when they think about each other, some when they part. There are many types. Even if I teach you a hundred a day, it'll take me almost twenty days to teach you all of them.

Tharlo: I don't need to learn so many. Why don't you teach me three that are sung when the couple first meet?

She laughs. Now I know why you want to learn the la glu. *Tharlo joins in laughing.*

Girl whose lower face is covered with a scarf: In such case I'll teach you three of the best ones.

Tharlo sits up on his motorbike. She clears her throat and sings: In the monasteries of Ü-Tsang / Pilgrims call the name of Siddhartha. / You must worship with sincerity. / Without a sincere heart / There is no reason to prostrate yourself. / Do not concern yourself with the affairs of the world. / Do not trifle with the holy Buddha. / In a village as wide as the sea / Two lovers give their hearts to one other. / If you want your love to bear fruits, / With a true heart / Spend your days in bringing me delight. / Do not make vows you cannot keep. / Do not trifle with me.

When she finishes she asks Tharlo: Do you like this one?

Tharlo replies: Yes, this one is good.

She suggests: I'll sing you one more.

Then she starts singing without having to think about it: In a monastery in Ü-Tsang / There is a master who lives in peace. / He keeps a Fumyo Sutra in the library. / Please open the door to the library. / The novice has come to read and study it. / In a quiet village / The one I love brings me peace of mind. / I keep the la glu in my heart. / Please come to open the door to my heart. / My beloved, I'm waiting for you.

Tharlo cries: This one won't do! This is sung by a woman to a man. I need one that is sung by a man to a woman.

The girl whose lower face is covered with a scarf laughs. Alright, I see.

She clears her throat and sings: On the turquoise-tinted grassland / Horses gallop in pairs. / I am the only one without company. / Fair mare, come gallop by my side! / In the village of our tribe / Lovers go in pairs. / I am the only one all alone. / Fair maid, be my companion!

She says to him: What about this one?

Tharlo: This is a good one.

Girl whose lower face is covered with a scarf: Twenty yuan now.

Tharlo: Fine, fine. Twenty, twenty.

Girl whose lower face is covered with a scarf: I'll sing another one.

Tharlo: Good, another one.

She clears her throat and sings: I may not be the fastest steed / But with my rein in your hand in front / And a whip on my rump behind, / I have no choice but to gallop on. / I may not be the greatest lover / But with my name uttered in your sweet voice / and the honey dripping from your words, / I have no choice but to say I love you.

When she finishes the song, she asks Tharlo: What about this one?

Tharlo: This one is very good.

Girl whose lower face is covered with a scarf: Thirty yuan.

Tharlo: Fine, fine. Thirty.

Girl whose lower face is covered with a scarf: Do you want to hear another one?

Tharlo: That's fine for the time being. Let's sing more another day.

Girl whose lower face is covered with a scarf: Can you remember everything?

Tharlo: I can. I have a good memory.

Girl whose lower face is covered with a scarf: Yes, I can well believe it.

Tharlo takes out thirty yuan from his pocket, and puts it under a rock. I'll leave thirty yuan here. Pick it up from here.

Girl whose lower face is covered with a scarf: I was joking. All I did was to teach you three la glu!

Tharlo sees that his sheep have gone far. I'll leave it here for you. I've got to go after my sheep. *Tharlo starts his motorbike and rides off.*

The girl whose lower face is covered with a scarf slowly walks over to where Tharlo was. She picks up the money, and looks towards Tharlo. After a while she calls toward him: I almost forgot! Your employer has sent word. He'll send his son over in a couple of days for some sheep dung. He tells you to prepare it.

Tharlo looks back at her.

Scene 35   Sheep pen. Exterior. Evening.

Tharlo gathers sheep dung in the sheep pen. He piles the sheep dung, and carries it outside the pen. Then he spreads out the sheep dung to dry. When he finishes, he drives the sheep back into the pen.

Scene 29   **Tharlo's mountain shed. Interior. Night.**

Shot 42   *Close-up of radio in Tharlo's hand.*

[Tharlo is lying on the platform-bed listening to la glu in the radio.]

The song on the radio: High in the mountains / Birds fly in pairs. / I have no one to fly together with. / Come and fly by my side! / Vast are the lands in this world. / In pairs are those who know each other's heart. / I am yet to find my companion. / Fair maid! / Come and keep me company ...

Scene 30   **Outside Tharlo's mountain shed. Exterior. Night.**

Shot 43   *Extreme wide shot. Tharlo's shed is on the right. The moon is visible in the sky but extremely small. The barking of a dog is occasionally heard.*

Scene 31   **Outside sheep pen. Exterior. Day.**

Shot 44   *Full shot. Tharlo comes out of his shed towards his dog in the foreground.*

[Tharlo brings food to his dog. He squats down in front of it and watches him eat.]

Scene 32   **Sheep pen. Exterior. Day.**

Shot 45   *Medium shot. Tharlo on the right-hand side of the frame.*

[Tharlo gathers sheep dung in the pen, then sweeps it all into a burlap sack.]

Shot 46   *Wide shot from high angle. Tharlo on the right. On his left, opposite, is a scarecrow.*

[Tharlo spreads out the sheep dung to dry.]

Scene 36   Outside sheep pen. Exterior. Night.

Tharlo lights a double-blast firecracker, then cries out into the dark night.

Scene 37   Tharlo's mountain shed. Interior. Morning.

Close-up on the alarm clock. It goes off.

Scene 38   By the stream. Exterior. Day.

Tharlo drives the sheep to drink in the stream. He pours water into a vessel, and raises the bucket and drinks from it. The sheep are also drinking. A ewe looks at Tharlo. He holds the little lamb in his arms.

He starts singing to the ewe one of the la glu the girl whose lower face is covered with a scarf taught him: I may not be the fastest steed / But with my rein in your hand in front / And a whip on my rump behind, / I have no choice but to gallop on. / I may not be the greatest lover / But with my name uttered in your sweet voice / and the honey dripping from your words, / I have no choice but to say I love you.

Tharlo's expression and voice are both strange when he sings the la glu. The ewe listens to him singing the whole song, then walks away. He watches her walk away.

Scene 33   At the well. Exterior. Day.

Shot 47   Extreme wide shot. Tharlo in the middle with over a hundred sheep around him.

Tharlo [*singing a la glu he's learnt from the radio as he gets water from the well for the sheep to drink*] Let's sing a love song! / Fair maiden! / High in the mountains / Birds fly in pairs.

Shot 48   Wide shot. Side view of Tharlo with sheep around him.

Tharlo: [*continuing to sing*] I have no one to fly together with. / Come and fly by my side!

Tharlo: [*sitting down, still among the sheep, and continuing to sing*] Let's sing a love song! / Fair maiden!

Shot 49-51   Close-up on the face of a sheep in each shot. Tharlo's singing continues to be heard as voice-over.

Tharlo: [*continuing to sing*] Vast are the lands in this world. / In pairs are those who know each other's heart. / I am yet to find my companion. / Fair maiden! / Come and keep me company!

Shot 52   Wide shot. Tharlo is sitting with his back to the camera, still singing.

[*Tharlo stops singing, and smokes. The bleating and bells of the sheep are heard, then they quickly become faint echoes. The sheep walk away from where he sits.*]

Scene 39   Outside the sheep pen. Exterior. Early evening.

Tharlo puts the dried sheep dung into a burlap sack. Several burlap sacks that have been filled lie around on the ground.

Scene 40   Tharlo's mountain shed. Interior. Night.

Tharlo eats the barley cakes as he rubs yak butter into the barley flour. When he finishes, he takes a shred of newspaper and carefully rolls a cigarette with it. Then he lights his cigarette and smokes, deep in thought. Suddenly he coughs. A paroxysm of his recurrent cough seizes him. He stands up to get a bottle of wine. He pours down half a bottle in a couple of swigs. Then he stares at the fire in the stove. The fire is burning red. He picks up some double-blast firecrackers, and goes outside.

Scene 41   Outside the sheep pen. Exterior. Night.

Tharlo lights the firecrackers. Then he cries out in the dark after the sharp crack of the firecrackers.

Scene 34   **Outside the sheep pen. Exterior. Early evening.**

Shot 53   *Wide shot. Tharlo is sitting on the ground with his back to the camera, with a scarecrow to his right. Just in front are his motorbike and a few burlap sacks of sheep dung lying around. Further ahead is a high-voltage pylon with electric cables running through it. Faint ringing of sheep bells can still be heard.*

Scene 35   **Tharlo's mountain shed. Interior. Night.**

Shot 54   *Medium shot. Frontal view of Tharlo sitting on the floor in front of the wall. To his left is the iron stove. Something is steaming on it to provide warmth.*

[Tharlo lights his cigarette and smokes, sunk deep in thought. Suddenly he coughs. A paroxysm of his recurrent cough seizes him. He walks to the right and out of the frame. When he enters the frame again, he has a bottle of rice wine in his hand. He gulps down half a bottle in a couple of swigs.]

Scene 36   **Outside Tharlo's mountain shed. Exterior. Night.**

Shot 55   *Extreme wide shot. In the middle of the mountain in the pitch dark night the light of Tharlo's mountain shed comes through the door and the window. From the moving light beam from his hand torch one can make out the tiny moving figure of Tharlo in front of the shed.*

[Tharlo lights the firecrackers. Distant bursts from the explosion of firecrackers are seen. Then he cries out in the dark following the sharp crack of firecrackers.]

Scene 37   **Tharlo's mountain shed. Interior. Night.**

Shot 56   *Full shot. Tharlo is asleep with his upper body leaning against the wall. An empty wine bottle and a few items in front of him.*

Scene 42   Tharlo's mountain shed. Interior. Morning.

The alarm clock goes off.

Scene 43   Sheep pen. Exterior. Morning.

Tharlo comes outside from the shed. It is very quiet. He looks at where the dog is supposed to be. It is gone. He walks to the sheep pen. He is very nervous.

A dozen sheep carcasses are lying around. The other sheep in the pen are extremely frightened. They all stand under the wall pressing themselves to each other. The carcasses are all mutilated by the wolves' fangs. Shreds of flesh and bloodstains are visible.

Tharlo's little lamb has also been killed by the wolves. Its body is lying on the ground.

Tharlo is in shock. He stands there, not knowing what to do. The sun is slowly rising. It shines on the dead body of the little lamb. There is dark blood staining the ground around it. Tharlo picks it up. Then he sits among the sheep carcasses, and weeps.

A tractor is coming this way on the dirt road from a distance. It arrives at the sheep pen.

The driver stands on the edge of the pen, shocked by what he sees in front of him.

The tractor has stopped moving, but the engine is still running. The noise it makes is audible.

[Tharlo is holding the radio close to him, and has fallen asleep by the stove. The radio is playing a la glu.]

Song from the radio: I might not be the fastest stallion. / If you can kindly set a saddle for me, / I still won't fly in the sky like a bird, / but I'll gallop faster than the wind.

Shot 57   Medium shot. A painting on the wall with two butter lamps and other sacrifice in front of it. The la glu from the radio continues.

Song from the radio: I might not be the sweetest talking lover. / If you make a commitment to me, / even if I can't protect you in the next life, / I'll always watch over you in this life.

[One after another, the lamps slowly burn out.]

Scene 38   Sheep pen. Exterior. Morning.

Shot 58   Wide shot. Carcasses of sheep are scattered about. Tharlo enters frame in the background at the edge of the sheep pen. He approaches the middle of the frame as he walks further into the pen.

[A dozen sheep carcasses are lying around. The remaining sheep in the pen are all extremely frightened. They stand under the wall pressing themselves to each other. Tharlo's little lamb has also been killed by the wolves. Its body is lying on the ground. Tharlo picks it up and holds it close to his chest. The sheep exit the pen from the gate in the background that Tharlo has left open.]

Shot 59   Full shot. Tharlo sits by the wall with the body of the lamb on his lap. The engine of a tractor is heard in the distance.

Shot 60   Extreme wide shot. A tractor is proceeding under a high voltage pylon towards the direction where Tharlo's motorbike is parked.

Shot 61   Wide shot. Tharlo sits in the foreground on the left by a mud wall outside his shed. The entrance to the sheep pen is behind the mud wall. On the higher ground on the right is a scarecrow.

[The driver walks into the frame towards Tharlo, and stands in front of him.

The driver comes to stand in front of Tharlo. Tharlo stands up. The driver stares at Tharlo's face, and slaps him. Did you get drunk again?

Tharlo doesn't say anything. There is no expression on his face.

The driver takes out a bottle of rice wine from his bag, and presses it to Tharlo. A drink for you!

Tharlo doesn't take it. The driver throws it on a rock next to their feet to smash it. The bottle is shattered. The wine flows out.

The driver says in a cold voice: Don't you know you are a shepherd? *Tharlo doesn't say anything. There is still no expression on his face.*

The driver slaps him again. Remember, you tend sheep. *Still Tharlo doesn't say anything, or show any emotion.*

Tharlo and the driver start lifting the sacks of sheep dung onto the tractor. When that is done, they lift the sheep carcasses onto the tractor. Then the driver picks one of the carcasses from the tractor and throws it onto the ground. This one is for you to eat.

Then he says: As for the sheep killed by wolves, count the loss as yours.

Tharlo doesn't say anything. The tractor drives slowly away along the dirt road. Tharlo watches it depart, with no expression on his face.

Tharlo hangs the sheep carcass on a wooden pole to skin it. He holds a knife between his teeth, and pulls out the guts of the sheep. His mouth and hands are stained with blood.

Tharlo makes no response. The driver goes into the sheep pen, and looks around. All this is done with his back to the camera.]

Shot 62   Medium shot. Tharlo and driver stand facing each other in front of the mud wall. Side view of the two men. A couple of sheep carcasses are hanging from the higher ground of the sheep pen on the other side of the mud wall.

[The driver stares at Tharlo's face, and slaps him.]

Driver: Did you get drunk again?

[Tharlo doesn't say anything. There is no expression on his face. The driver takes out a bottle of rice wine from his bag, and presses it to Tharlo.]

Driver: A drink for you!

[Tharlo doesn't take it. The driver drops the bottle on the ground to smash it. He lights a cigarette for himself, and keeps staring at Tharlo's face, then slaps him again. Tharlo doesn't respond.]

Driver: *[in a cold voice]* Don't you know you are a shepherd?

[Tharlo doesn't say anything. There is still no expression on his face. The driver slaps him again.]

Driver: Remember, you tend sheep.

[Still Tharlo doesn't say anything, or show any emotion.]

Shot 63   Medium shot featuring the face of the driver, now back in the tractor, in the wing mirror. In the background Tharlo is carrying the sheep carcasses and putting them onto the tractor. The driver starts the tractor to drive away.

Shot 64   Wide shot. The tractor begins to drive off carrying the carcasses in the back, while Tharlo stands watching with his back to the camera. To his left is an old prayer flag.

[The tractor stops. The driver picks one of the carcasses from the tractor, and throws it onto the ground.]

Driver: This one is for you to eat. As for these sheep killed by wolves, count the loss as yours.

Scene 44   Tharlo's mountain shed. Interior. Night.

The stove fire is burning high. The mutton is cooking in the pan. It is steaming. The noise of the pan boiling is clearly audible. Tharlo starts to eat the mutton. He drinks rice wine. His facial expression is indistinct. When he finishes eating, he takes out all the remaining firecrackers.

Scene 45   Outside the sheep pen. Exterior. Night.

Tharlo lights many firecrackers outside his shed. He cries as loudly as he can as he lights them. This lasts for a long time.

Black screen. Suddenly everything goes quiet. There is no more sound.

Scene 46   On the grassland. Exterior. Morning.

The sun is rising slowly. Tharlo sits on the grassland, with his back to the camera. There are a few high-voltage electricity pylons in front of him. The cables extend into the distance. Tharlo looks ahead of him. After a while he gets up, and turns. He walks towards a nettle-bush, takes out a match, and sets it on fire. The nettles are burning. Tharlo stretches his hand towards the fire to warm them. His hands are now extremely close to the fire. They are almost burnt by the fire. Tharlo looks lost.

[Tharlo doesn't say anything. The tractor drives slowly away along the dirt road.]

Shot 65   Medium overhead shot of Tharlo pulling out the entrails of the
                 dead sheep. Its belly is slit wide open, with its guts clearly visible.

Scene 39   Tharlo's mountain shed. Interior. Night.

Shot 66   *Medium shot of steaming pan on stove.*

*[The stove is on a high flame and the mutton is cooking in the steaming pot. The
sound of the boiling pot is clearly audible. Tharlo sits down, starts to eat the
mutton, and drinks rice wine.]*

Scene 40   On the grassland. Exterior. Morning.

Shot 67   *Wide shot. Dim light before dawn. A figure can be seen sitting
                 with his back to the camera.*

*[Tharlo gets up and walks towards a nettle-bush, takes out a match, and sets
it on fire. The nettles blaze. Tharlo stretches his hands towards the fire to
warm them. Very quiet sustained notes on synthesizer as non-diegetic sound
track underscores the diegetic noise of burning nettles.]*

Scene 47   County town. Exterior. Dusk.

Tharlo is riding his motorbike on the streets of the county township. The satchel on his back looks full. He fixes his eyes ahead. There is a vacuous expression on his face. A police car passes him by. He doesn't seem to notice it, and keeps driving ahead. A policeman pops his head out of the car window, and shouts a curse at Tharlo.

Tharlo arrives at the barbershop. He stops the motorbike outside the door, looks in through the glass window, then enters.

Scene 48   Barbershop. Interior. Dusk.

The shorthaired girl is cutting a man's hair. Tharlo sits down on a stool on one side. He looks at her in the mirror. She gives him a smile, also in the mirror, without turning to greet him.

When the man is gone, she says to Tharlo, still in the mirror: Your hair is dirty again. It's time for another wash.

He walks over and sits in the chair the other man just sat in, then looks at her in the mirror. Now she can see him clearly, and says: What's happened to you? You look so pale!

He puts his satchel on top of her box of hairdressing appliances. Then he goes to shut the door, and comes back to sit in the barber's chair. He takes out bundles of money from his satchel, and leaves them on the worktop in front of him. Then he sits back in the barber's chair, and slowly he says: There's one hundred sixty thousand yuan here.

The shorthaired girl looks at the money, very surprised. Tharlo looks at her in the mirror. The girl looks back at him in the mirror. He looks nervous, his chest heaves as he breathes.

She places both hands on his shoulder, and looks at his pale face in the mirror. Relax. Relax. Everything will be fine once you relax.

He is silent and looks pale. The shorthaired girl says: Let me drywash your hair. *Tharlo responds with a faint 'right'.*

She squeezes out some shampoo and gently rubs it into his hair. He gradually

Scene 41   A street. Exterior. Day.

Shot 68   *Wide shot of Tharlo riding his motorbike on a busy street. It is the same street in the township as in Shot 23, but filmed from the opposite direction. Street bustle and traffic noise.*

Scene 42   Barbershop. Interior. Dusk.

Shot 69   *Medium shot. Filmed as mirror reflection. Tharlo is sitting in the barber's chair in front of the mirror. The shorthaired girl stands behind him. Some decorative fairy lights on the wall to the right of the mirror are flashing.*

[Tharlo takes out bundles of banknotes from his satchel, and leaves them on the worktop in front of him. Then he sits back in the barber's chair.]

Tharlo: *[slowly]* There's one hundred sixty thousand yuan here.

[The girl looks at the money, very surprised.]

Tharlo: Put it away. *[He looks nervous, his chest heaves as he breathes.]*

[The girl puts the money away. Then she walks back to stand behind him, and places both hands on his shoulder. She takes off his hat, and gently massages his head.]

Shorthaired girl: *[after a while]* Are you willing to do one more thing for the two of us? Your ponytail draws too much attention. Let's cut it. Without it no one will recognise you. Will you do that? If you like me with long hair, I'll grow it out for you. I'll keep two lovely plaits, just to please you. Will you do that?

[She looks at him in the mirror. He looks back at her. Then he closes his eyes, and nods. She wraps a towel around his shoulders, picks up her electric razor, and shaves his hair with exact and self-assured movements.

Tharlo becomes completely bald. He looks at himself in the mirror. He closes his eyes again.]

relaxes and slowly closes his eyes. The colour on his face comes back. He seems to have fallen asleep.

When he wakes up, she is sitting by his side looking at him. She says: You fell asleep.

He looks around with a dreamy expression on his face, and a dreamy look in his eyes. The shorthaired girl continues: I've tied up your ponytail nice and neat.

He continues to stare into the vacuum. She passes a bottle of drinking water to him. Have some water. *He unscrews the lid and takes a few sips.*

She looks into his eyes. Now, there's one more thing you need to do for the two of us.

He stares at her and takes another sip of water.

Shorthaired girl: Would you? *He takes a big sip of water and makes a gurgling noise in his throat as he swallows it. His throat feels unusually tight.*

Shorthaired girl: Your ponytail draws too much attention. You've got to cut it. *She continues:* Without it no one will recognise you.

Tharlo stops drinking the water and looks at himself in the mirror. She looks back at him in the mirror. You agree, right? *He continues to stare at his own face.*

Shorthaired girl: If you like me with long hair, I'll grow it out for you. I'll keep two lovely plaits, just to please you.

He looks at her again in the mirror. She continues: I'll cut it now. We'll shave it all off. Nobody will recognise you with a bald head.

Tharlo touches his own hair, then his ponytail. The expression on his face is strange. The girl looks at him in the mirror. Then he closes his eyes. She picks up her electric razor, and shaves his hair with exact and self-assured movements. Tharlo's ponytail falls by the girl's feet, still tied together by the red thread.

Tharlo becomes completely bald. He looks at himself in the mirror. He can hardy recognise himself.

The girl pulls open the curtain, and looks outside.

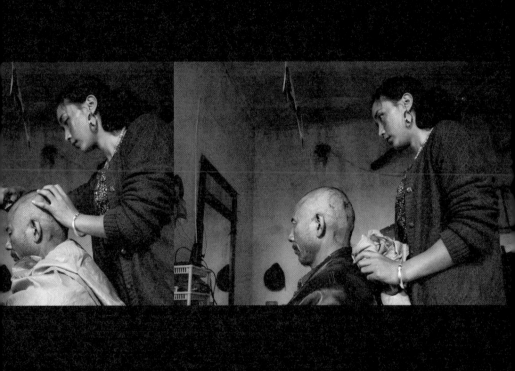

Scene 49   Street. Exterior. Dusk

Promotion broadcast outside is heard: Tonight, the famous singer Dekyi Tserang will perform in Norbu Lingka Club. This is too rare an opportunity to miss! *A small van covered in promotional banners is driving slowly past. On the banners are promotional graphics of Dekyi Tserang's gig. The broadcast comes from the loudspeakers on the roof of the van.*

Scene 50   Barbershop. Interior. Dusk.

Shorthaired girl: Let's go to the gig this evening.

Tharlo: Let's go to the place we sang last time. What is that place called?

Shorthaired girl: That was the karaoke bar. We'll go to that sort of place another night. We have all the time in the world now.

Tharlo: I've learnt a few la glu. I want to sing them to you.

She laughs. We'll be together every day now. Sing them to me some other day. This evening is the only chance to see the concert.

Tharlo: Alright.

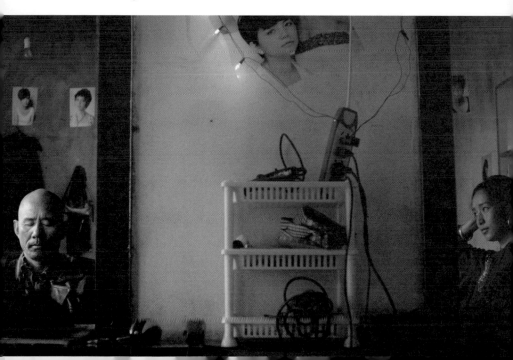

Shot 70   Full shot. Street outside is seen through the window frame.

[A van covered in promotional posters of Dekyi Tserang's gig is driving past outside the barbershop.]

Promotional broadcast from the van: Tonight, the famous singer Dekyi Tserang will perform in Norbu Lingka Club. Don't miss this exceptional opportunity!

Shot 71   Medium shot. Filmed as mirror reflection. Tharlo is seen on the
             left in mirror reflection sitting in the barber's chair with the
             shorthaired girl standing behind him. The same position and
             composition as Shot 69.

[Tharlo is nodding off, but he wakes up, and opens his eyes as he feels the girl bending down behind him. Her face is close to his.]

Shorthaired girl: Let's go to the gig this evening.

Tharlo: I don't want to. Let's go to the place where we sang last time. What is that place called?

Shorthaired girl: That was the karaoke bar. We'll go to that kind of place another night. We have all the time in the world now.

Tharlo: I've learnt a few la glu. I want to sing them to you.

Shorthaired girl: [laughing lightly]. We'll be together every day now. Sing them to me some other day. This evening is the only chance to see the concert.

Tharlo: Alright. [He closes his eyes again.]

[The shorthaired girl straightens up her body, looks at him in the mirror, and walks to the right. She is seen sitting down and reclining in a chair in the reflection of the mirror on the right, still looking at him. After a while she closes her eyes, too. Tharlo's singing of a la glu is faintly heard as voice over.]

Scene 51   Nightclub. Exterior. Night.

The neon sign outside the nightclub is flashing.

Scene 52   Nightclub. Interior. Night.

Tharlo and the shorthaired girl are sitting in a nightclub. The place is very crowded, noisy and smoky. Some people are already drunk. The shorthaired girl is smoking and drinking beer. She is laughing.

MC on stage: Let's give Dekyi Tserang a big hand, and let's cheer for him. He's going to sing us his most popular song!

The audience respond with loud applause, cheers and whistles. The shorthaired girl joins the cheering. Tharlo looks at her. The singer comes on stage and sings.

Tharlo: Let's go to that karaoke bar we went to last time. That place is better.

Shorthaired girl: Let's go there another night. Let's stay here tonight.

Tharlo: Let's go there. I want to sing you the la glu I've learnt.

Shorthaired girl: Didn't I say that we'd have all the time in the world? Let's stay here tonight. This is a rare chance to hear him.

Tharlo doesn't look willing. The shorthaired girl takes out a bottle of rice wine from her bag. I worry you might cough. So I've brought a bottle with me. Why don't you drink some? *She uses her teeth to open the lid, and passes the bottle to Tharlo. She picks up a beer and clinks it against Tharlo's rice wine. Tharlo raises his bottle to her, and takes a big sip.*

The singer just finishes his song. Tharlo watches the audience cheer.

Shorthaired girl: Do you like it?

Tharlo: Not at all. It's too noisy.

Shorthaired girl: You don't understand this kind of music.

Tharlo: I prefer the la glu.

Scene 43   Nightclub. Interior. Night.

Shot 72   *Wide shot. Singer on stage. The stage backdrop is a photo of the Potala Palace flanked on both sides by a life-sized photo of the singer.*

[The place is crowded. The audience are responding to the singer with loud applause, cheers and whistles.]

The singer: *[singing in rap style]* My dear father! / Burning inside the lonely tent / You're like a butter lamp that never burns out. / Your children present to you / A khata to show you respect. / The mulberry incense burns as a sacrifice on the mountain top. / Your children pray for you / Wishing you peace and safety. / The prayer banners flap in the wind. / Your children pray for you / wishing you luck and happiness. / My dear father! / I wish to become an eagle / That flies freely in your sky. / I wish to become a stallion/ That gallops freely on your grasslands. / You are the lamp that lights up my way in the dark night. / With you there I won't lose my way. / You are the sunshine that warms me in my journey. / With you there I won't lose myself. / Every moment. / Day and night.

Tharlo's voice: Let's go to that karaoke bar we went to last time. That place is better.

Shorthaired girl's voice: Let's go there another night. Let's stay here tonight.

Tharlo's voice: Let's go there. I want to sing you the la glu I've learnt.

Shorthaired girl's voice: Didn't I say that we'd have all the time in the world? Let's stay here tonight. This is a rare opportunity to hear him.

Shot 73   *Medium shot. Back of Tharlo's bald head and the girl's head in the audience.*

Shorthaired girl: *[taking out a bottle of rice wine from her bag]* I was worried

Shorthaired girl: Come on, drink up! *They drink.*

The singer on stage continues to sing. Tharlo is bored. He takes out some newspaper shreds and tobacco from his pocket, and rolls a cigarette. Then he lights it and smokes. The girl notices that he is making a roll-up. You can't smoke this here. The smell is too strong. Smoke one of mine.

Tharlo is a bit annoyed. I'll smoke this.

A young man comes towards them. He looks at the shorthaired girl and asks her: Yangtso, who is this?

Shorthaired girl: A friend of mine.

The young man looks at Tharlo, and says to him: Your bald head is cool!

Tharlo pays no attention to him. He takes a puff of his roll-up, and lets the smoke out through his nose. The young man smells the smoke. He laughs and says to Tharlo: Your cigarette will choke everybody here. Let me give you a good cigarette to smoke. *He takes a cigarette out from his pack of 'China Brand' and gives it to Tharlo.*

Tharlo does not take it, but takes another puff of his roll-up. The young man looks at Tharlo, and lights the cigarette for himself. Then he says to the shorthaired girl: Yangtso, come to have a drink with us.

Shorthaired girl: My friend is here tonight. I've got to keep him company.

The young man is slightly drunk. Come on, you also have to keep us company. *He grabs Yangtso's arm.*

Tharlo extinguishes the end of his roll-up, and pushes the young man away from the shorthaired girl. He asks her: Who is he?

The shorthaired girl looks uneasy. He's a friend of mine.

The young man gives Tharlo a push. What do you think you're doing?

Tharlo: You'd better get away from us, and leave Yangtso alone.

The young man laughs. Hey, hey! Who are you to Yangtso? Why do you think it's your business?

you might cough. So I've brought a bottle of rice wine with me. Why don't you drink some?

[Tharlo takes the bottle from her, and takes a big sip. The singer just finishes his song. The shorthaired girl joins in the cheering.]

Shot 74   *Wide shot. Singer on stage. Tharlo and the shorthaired girl sit at the table in the lower right-hand corner of the frame. Tharlo sits with his back to the camera.*

[Audience going up to place pieces of khata round the singer's neck.]

Shorthaired girl: Do you like it?

Tharlo: Not at all. It's too noisy.

Shorthaired girl: You don't understand this kind of music.

Tharlo: I prefer the la glu.

Shorthaired girl: Come on, drink up!

[The singer on stage continues to sing.]

Shot 75   *Medium shot. Tharlo and the shorthaired girl sit at the table with beer bottles in front of them. Side view.*

[Tharlo is bored. He takes out some newspaper shreds and tobacco from his pocket, and rolls a cigarette. Then he lights it and smokes. The shorthaired girl notices that he is making a roll-up.]

Shorthaired girl: You can't smoke this here. The smell is too strong. Smoke one of mine.

[Tharlo ignores her and continues smoking his roll-up. She lights a cigarette for herself. A man who is also smoking a cigarette comes to sit at their table.]

Man: *[looking at the shorthaired girl]* Who is this?

Shorthaired girl: A friend of mine.

Man: *[looking at Tharlo]* Your friend's bald head is cool!

[Tharlo pays no attention to them. He takes a puff of his roll-up.]

Tharlo charges at the young man. The shorthaired girl stops him. Let's go. Let's go to the karaoke bar. It's too noisy here.

She pulls Tharlo away, and they leave through the door of the nightclub.

Man: [smelling the smoke] Your cigarette will choke everybody here. Let me give you a good cigarette to smoke. [He gives Tharlo one of his own cigarettes. Tharlo does not take it, instead taking another puff of his roll-up. He looks at Tharlo, then turns to the shorthaired girl.] Yangtso, come to have a drink with us.

Shorthaired girl: My friend is here tonight. I've got to keep him company.

Man: You also have to keep us company. [He grabs the shorthaired girl's arm as he stands up.] Come on, just a few drinks.

[Tharlo grabs the man's hand to make him let go of the shorthaired girl.]

Man: [to Tharlo] Who are you? [to the shorthaired girl] Who is this man?

Shorthaired girl: [looking uneasy] He's a friend of mine.

Man: Who are you to Yangtso?

Tharlo: You'd better get away from us, and leave Yangtso alone.

Man: [pushing Tharlo back] And who do you think you are?

Shot 76   Wide shot. Yangtso is standing and Tharlo is sitting in the lower right-hand corner of the frame. In the centre is the singer on stage. Downstage around Yangtso and Tharlo are various audience-members sitting round tables.

[Tharlo stands up. The man goes to another table to call his gang of friends over. Tharlo and the men start pushing each other.]

Shorthaired girl: [stopping Tharlo from fighting] Let's go. Let's go to the karaoke bar. It's too noisy here.

[The shorthaired girl pulls Tharlo away. Tharlo is pushed away from their table. He and the shorthaired girl retreat towards the foreground and exit the frame on the left.]

Scene 53   Barbershop. Interior. Morning.

Tharlo wakes up, and finds himself in the shorthaired girl's bed again. He looks to his side. The girl isn't there. He looks around. He sees nothing but a few household items scattered on the floor. He suddenly thinks of something, and rushes back to the bed, and looks for his satchel. He finds his satchel, but the money inside is gone. He looks everywhere, and rummages several times through the work counter in front of the barber's chair. He can't find what he's looking for.

He half sits and half collapses on the edge of the bed.

Scene 54   Karaoke bar. Exterior. Day.

Tharlo on his motorbike. He arrives at the karaoke bar. He stops, and enters the bar.

Scene 55   Karaoke bar. Interior. Day.

Tharlo rushes into the bar. He wakes the waiter who has put his head on the counter and slept. He asks him whether he has seen the shorthaired girl who was with him last night. The waiter says no, and is angry with Tharlo for waking him.

Scene 44   **Barbershop. Interior. Morning.**

Shot 77   *Medium shot. Filmed as mirror reflection. An iron stove is in the centre of the frame with a kettle on top. To the right Tharlo's lower body under a blanket is seen stretched out on the sofa. The composition is the reverse of Shot 22.*

[Tharlo wakes up, and finds himself on the shorthaired girl's sofa again. He looks to his side. The girl isn't there. He looks around but can't see her. He suddenly thinks of something. He checks the drawer in which the shorthaired girl put the money. The money is gone.]

Shot 78   *Wide shot. The sign and door of Dekyi Photo Studio on the opposite street is seen through the glass window of the barbershop. Sound of opening and closing drawers.*

Scene 45   **Karaoke bar. Interior. Day.**

Shot 79   *Wide shot. Cashier counter in the karaoke bar. The place is dark. Loud knocking on the door.*

[The knocking wakes the waiter who has put his head on the counter and slept. He goes out of the frame on the right. Sound of opening door. Light comes through from the same direction.]

Tharlo's voice: Have you seen the girl who was here with me last night?

Waiter 's voice: Which girl?

Tharlo's voice: The one with short hair.

Waiter's voice: No. We aren't open yet. Go away.

Scene 56   County town. Exterior. Day.

Tharlo goes all over town looking for the girl. He passes street after street, driving fast.

He arrives on his motorbike outside Dekyi Photo Studio, gets off, and enters.

Scene 57   Dekyi Photo Studio. Interior. Day.

Tharlo hurries into the studio, and asks Dekyi: Have you seen the shorthaired girl?

Dekyi is surprised by this. What shorthaired girl?

Tharlo. The shorthaired girl of the barbershop opposite. Her name is Yangtso.

Dekyi: Oh, her. I don't know. She comes and goes. I don't know where she is.

Tharlo: Where is her hometown?

Dekyi: Who would know that?

Tharlo says no more.

Dekyi: What has happened?

Tharlo leaves the studio.

Scene 58   Outside the Barbershop. Exterior. Day.

Tharlo sits on his motorbike, and looks at the barbershop with its door locked and curtains drawn. He rides away.

Scene 46   **A street. Exterior. Day.**

Shot 80   *Wide shot of the street filmed as reflection in the rear view mirror of a vehicle parked in the street.*

[Tharlo is driving around to look for the shorthaired girl.]

Shot 81   *Wide shot filmed through the glass window of the barbershop on the opposite street. The same position as Shot 12 but not reversed as mirror reflection. There is a truck with a full load in the foreground. It drives away to reveal Tharlo arriving at the photo studio on the opposite side of the street on his motorbike.*

[Tharlo gets off his motorbike and enters. After a while he comes back out of the photo studio, looks at the barbershop from the opposite side of the street, starts the motorbike and turns to stop in front of the barbershop before driving away.]

Scene 59   On the road. Exterior. Day.

Tharlo is riding back in the direction of the mountain. (Suggestion: Shooting on the Chabcha Airport runway.)

Scene 60   Township police station. Interior. Day.

The police chief and a few policemen are busy working. Tharlo pushes the door open.

Tharlo: Chief Dorje. It's me.

The police chief gives him a long hard look, finally recognising him. Ponytail! What have you done to yourself? Where is your ponytail?

Tharlo: I had it cut.

Police chief: What a pity.

Tharlo: Chief, do you think I look like a bad person now?

Police chief: What do you mean?

Tharlo: Isn't it true that you can tell a good person from a bad one with a single glance?

The police chief smiles. The only time you might have looked a little bit like a bad person was when you had your ponytail, but now you don't look anything at all like a bad person. You look like an absolutely good person.

Tharlo: I'm afraid my death will be lighter than a feather.

The police chief is still smiling. So, do you want to recite the works of Chairman Mao again? I've heard what you can do with your memory trick. You don't have to repeat it.

Tharlo: It's such a pity. I can no longer 'die a death weightier than Mount Tai', just like Zhang Side did for the people. I can only 'die a death lighter

Scene 47   **A road. Exterior. Day.**

Shot 82   *Extreme wide shot. Tharlo is riding his motorbike behind barbed wire in the foreground. He is heading in the direction of the mountain. It is the same road as the one in Shot 25, but filmed from a different angle.*

Scene 48   **Police station. Interior. Day.**

Shot 83   *Medium shot. Filmed as mirror reflection. The slogan 'Serve the People' is prominent in its reverse image. The police chief and a policewoman are sitting opposite each other at their desks with the stove pipe in the foreground creating the effect of a partition between them. Side view.*

Tharlo: *[as he enters]* Chief Dorje.

Police chief: *[giving him a long and hard look]* Take off your hat. *[Tharlo takes his hat off.]*

Police chief: *[laughing]* What have you done to yourself? Where is your ponytail?

Tharlo: I had it cut off.

Police chief: What a pity.

Tharlo: Chief Dorje, do you think I look like a bad person now?

Police chief: What do you mean?

Tharlo: Isn't it true that you can tell a good person from a bad one with a single glance?

Police chief: *[smiling]* The only time you might have looked a little bit like a bad person was when you had your ponytail, but now you don't look anything at all like a bad person. You look like an absolutely good person.

Tharlo: I'm afraid my death will be lighter than a feather.

than a feather', like those bad people 'who work for the fascists, and die for the exploiters and oppressors'. *(These fragments of quotation are spoken in Tibetan.)*

The police chief smiles. This time you understand Chairman Mao better.

Tharlo keeps saying: What a shame!

The police chief smiles. Then he turns to the other policemen: Hey, can you believe it? This guy can recite by heart many passages from the works of Chairman Mao?

They stop what they are doing and look at Tharlo sceptically, as if to say: Him?

The police chief says: So, now we have to show you! *He turns to Tharlo.* Why don't you recite 'Serve the People' in Chinese? Show them!

Tharlo looks at the expressions of the policemen. Without paying any more attention to them he starts reciting: 'Serve the People.' Eighth of September, nineteen forty-four. Mao Zedong. Our Communist Party and the Eighth Route and New Fourth Armies led by our Party are battalions of our revolution. These battalions of ours are wholly dedicated to the liberation of the people and work entirely in the people's interests. Comrade Zhang Side was in the ranks of these battalions.

Suddenly Tharlo can't remember any more, but then he resumes: All men must die, but death can vary in its significance. The ancient Chinese writer Sima Qian said, 'Though death befalls all men alike, it may be weightier than Mount Tai or lighter than a feather.' To die for the people is weightier than Mount Tai, but to work for the fascists and die for the exploiters and oppressors is lighter than a feather. Comrade Zhang Side died for the people, and his death is indeed weightier than Mount Tai . . . *The policemen look at Tharlo in amazement.*

Tharlo stops. He opens his mouth, but no more words come out.

Police chief: Go on, why do you stop?

Tharlo opens his mouth several times, still no words come out.

Police chief: What is it with you today?

Police chief: So, do you want to recite the works of Chairman Mao again? I've heard you before. You don't have to repeat it.

Tharlo: It's such a pity. I can no longer 'die a death weightier than Mount Tai', just like Zhang Side did for the people. I can only 'die a death lighter than a feather', like those bad people 'who work for the fascists, and die for the exploiters and oppressors'. *[The above fragments of quotation are spoken in Tibetan]*

Police chief: *[smiling]* This time you understand Chairman Mao better. *[turning to the policemen, and speaking in Chinese]* Hey, can you believe it? This guy can recite by heart many passages from the works of Chairman Mao in Chinese? *[pause]* You don't believe me, do you? Come over, we'll show you. *[turning to Tharlo]* Why don't you recite 'Serve the People' in Chinese in full, just like you did the other day? Show them!

Tharlo: *[looking at the expressions of the policemen, and without paying any more attention to them]* 'Serve the People.' Eighth of September, nineteen forty-four. Mao Zedong. Our Communist Party and the Eighth Route and New Fourth Armies led by our Party are battalions of our revolution. These battalions of ours are wholly dedicated to the liberation of the people, and work entirely in the people's interests. Comrade Zhang Side was in the ranks of these battalions.

[Suddenly Tharlo can't remember any more. He thinks hard, then he continues.]

Tharlo: All men must die, but death can vary in its significance. The ancient Chinese writer Sima Qian said, 'Though death befalls all men alike, it may be weightier than Mount Tai or lighter than a feather.' To die for the people is weightier than Mount Tai, but to work for the fascists and die for the exploiters and oppressors is lighter than a feather. Comrade Zhang Side died for the people, and his death is indeed weightier than Mount Tai . . .

[He stops.]

Policemen: *[looking at their chief]* Chief, not like what you said.

Police chief: He wasn't like this a few days ago. He recited the entire 'Serve the People' speech in Chinese from beginning to end without a single pause. *[to Tharlo]* What is it with you today?

Tharlo doesn't know what to say, so he replies: I don't know. I can't remember the rest.

The policemen look at their chief. The police chief says: He wasn't like this a few days ago. He recited the entire 'Serve the People' speech from beginning to end without a single pause.

Tharlo starts coughing. The cough becomes so violent that his face turns red. He can't stop it.

The policemen look at Tharlo, rather disappointed.

Police chief: Well, let's get back to work. We haven't got much time to lose.

Tharlo says as he continues to cough: Chief Dorje, I've become a bad person now.

The police chief looks at him. You don't become a bad person just because you've shaved your head. *Then he says to one of the policemen:* Check those new identity cards, and find his.

The policeman asks: What's his name?

Police chief: Ponytail.

Policeman: Really?

Police chief: No, that's his nickname.

He turns to Tharlo: What's your real name?

Tharlo answers: Tharlo.

Police chief: Yes, now I remember. You're Tharlo.

The policeman searches for Tharlo's card in the filing cabinet. The police chief suddenly thinks of something. Yes, where is the little lamb you carried with you last time?

Tharlo: It was killed by wolves.

Police chief: Are the wolves near you so terrible?

Tharlo: Yes, they are.

Tharlo: I don't know. I just can't remember.

Police chief: *[laughing]* He isn't quite right today. Let's get back to work. We haven't got time to waste.

[The other policemen return to their desks.]

Tharlo: Chief Dorje, I've become a bad person now.

Police chief: You don't become a bad person just because you've shaved your head. *[to one of the policemen]* Check those new identity cards, and find his.

[The policeman walks over to search for Tharlo's card in the filing cabinet which is out of frame.]

Police chief: *[suddenly thinking of something]* Yes, where is the little lamb you carried with you last time?

Tharlo: It was killed by wolves.

Police chief: Are the wolves near you so terrible?

Tharlo: Yes, they are.

Policeman's voice: Chief, What's his name?

Police chief: Ponytail.

Policeman's voice: Really?

Police chief: No, that's his nickname. *[to Tharlo]* What is your real name?

Tharlo: Tharlo.

Police chief: Yes, Tharlo. Now I remember. *[taking up the issue about the wolves again]* In such case I have to report it to the higher authorities. We need to organise a hunt to eliminate them.

Policeman *[coming over with an identity card]* Chief, is this him? Now the photo doesn't look anything like him.

Police chief: *[taking a good look at the card, then at Tharlo]* This doesn't look like you. Are you planning to grow a ponytail again?

Police chief: In such case I have to report it to the higher authorities. We need to organise a hunt to eliminate them.

The policeman comes over with an identity card. Chief, is this him? Now the photo doesn't look anything like him.

The police chief takes a good look at the card. Then he turns to Tharlo. Are you planning to grow a ponytail again?

Tharlo: No.

Police chief: Then you've got to go into town again and get a new photo. This photo doesn't look like you. People who see your identity card won't be able to tell it's the same person.

Tharlo is still coughing. He is on the point of saying something but the cough stops him. The police chief gently pushes him out as he says: Go and come back as soon as you have the photo. We're very busy today.

Tharlo still wants to say something, but the police chief has already pushed him out. Tharlo is now outside the office but still facing it. The police chief shuts the door.

Scene 61   Outside the police station. Exterior. Day.

Tharlo exits from the side door on the second floor of the police station, and walks down the stairs slowly.

Scene 62   Outside a grocery store. Exterior. Day.

Tharlo enters the frame riding his motorbike. He stops, parks it, and enters the grocery store. After a while he comes out, drives away and out of frame.

Tharlo: No.

Police chief: Then you've got to go into town again and get a new photo. This photo doesn't look like you. People who see your identity card won't be able to tell it's the same person. Go on.

Tharlo: Chief Dorje…

Police chief: Go on! Off you go, and come back as soon as you have the photo. We're very busy today.

[Tharlo still wants to say something, but the police chief has already pushed him out. The policemen go back to sit at their desks, and resume working.]

Scene 49   Outside the police station. Exterior. Day.

Shot 84   Medium shot. A sign indicating 'Police' above the door of the police office.

[Tharlo walks through the door, turns back to look at it once again before walking away and exiting the frame on the right.]

Scene 50   Mountain road. Exterior. Day.

Shot 85   Extreme wide shot.

[Tharlo on his motorbike riding in the direction of the mountains with his back to the camera. A lorry comes up behind him. As it gets close, the sharp noise of the vehicle braking is heard. The lorry changes to the fast lane.]

Scene 63   Grassland. Exterior. Day.

Tharlo sits on his motorbike. His eyes are fixed on the horizon. He looks lost. There are many strange-shaped rocks surrounding him.

He slowly takes a double-blast firecracker out from his satchel, and lights it with a lighter. The firecracker explodes still in his palm.

He is still holding the firecracker in his grip. His hand is shaking. Blood seeps out from between his fingers.

Slowly he opens his hand. The flesh of his palm has been ripped open by the blast. The sight is bloody.

With the other hand he takes out a bottle of rice wine from his satchel. With much difficulty he takes off the lid with his teeth. He pours some wine onto his palm. His hand is shaking. His face is expressionless. He simply endures the pain.

He raises the bottle and takes a big swig of the rice wine. His eyes look vacuous.

He takes another swig and empties half of the bottle. Then he throws the bottle onto a rock. It breaks. The sound of breaking glass is audible. The wine flows out of the bottle, and seeps onto the stones. Then the stones dry in the sun.

Tharlo's face bears a helpless and confused expression.

VO of sheep bleating. Tharlo looks in the direction of the sheep.

Shot 86   Extreme wide shot.

[Tharlo continues on the road. After a bend in the road he stops. The sound of him repeatedly trying to start the engine of the motorbike is heard. He starts pushing the motorbike on foot.]

Scene 51   Grassland. Exterior. Day.

Shot 87   Full shot featuring Tharlo sitting on his motorbike in the foreground, side-on facing away from the camera.

[Tharlo sits on his motorbike. He is smoking. He takes out a bottle of rice wine from his satchel, and takes off the lid with his teeth. He takes a big swig of the rice wine, then another swig to empty half of the bottle. He throws the bottle onto the ground. It breaks. The sound of breaking glass is audible.

He coughs a little, takes a double-blast firecracker out from his satchel, and lights it with his cigarette. He stretches his arm to hold it in his palm away from himself. He looks at it and waits for it to explode.

Cut to black. Two sounds of firecracker exploding.]

Illustrations